TEACHING FUNDAMENTALS OF VIOLIN PLAYING

BY JACK M. PERNECKY

CONTRIBUTING EDITOR:
LORRAINE FINK

SUMMY-BIRCHARD INC.

© 1998 SUMMY-BIRCHARD MUSIC
DIVISION OF SUMMY-BIRCHARD, INC.
ALL RIGHTS RESERVED. PRINTED IN USA
ISBN 0-87487-771-7

SUMMY-BIRCHARD, INC.
EXCLUSIVELY DISTRIBUTED BY
WARNER BROS. PUBLICATIONS
15800 N.W. 48TH AVENUE
MIAMI, FLORIDA 33014

CONTENTS

Preface 5

Overview of Contents 6

Chapter 1: The Preparatory Period: Developing Basic Bowing Techniques;
Playing Posture and Left Hand Position; Bow and Left Hand Together; Dalcroze
Eurhythmics and Influence on Left Hand and Bowing Techniques 9

Chapter 2: Exercises in Developing Control and Flexibility in
the Bow Hold and in Bowing Movements 41

Chapter 3: Developing Left Hand and Finger Dexterity From
Beginning Movements to Advanced Trills 55

Chapter 4: Interrelating Repertoire with Scales, Mini-Exercises and Etudes 65

Chapter 5: The Scale: Building Techniques and Musical Skills 85

Chapter 6: Teaching Change of Position 95

Chapter 7: Teaching the Vibrato from Beginning to Advanced Levels 108

Chapter 8: Bowing Articulations 120

Chapter 9: Teaching and Practicing 133

Chapter 10: Playing Double Stops and Chords 141

Chapter 11: Private Studio and Classroom String Teaching Programs: Alternatives 149

Chapter 12: Keeping Interest Alive (Motivating Students) 158

Chapter 13: Learning Music Through Musical Form 163

Chapter 14: Creating an Effective Pedagogy 168

Resources: A. The Dalcroze Influence on String Pedagogy 172

B. Pizzicato Playing 173

C. Chinrests, Shoulder Rests and Pads 174

D. Parts of Violin and Bow 178

E. Glossary of Terms Used in Text 179

References 182

ACKNOWLEDGEMENTS

A special note of appreciation to Lorraine Fink, an outstanding teacher, who served as contributing editor and added valuable pedagogical ideas. Her expertise in Suzuki principles became an important part of this text. To Art Montzka, for his extraordinary ability in photographing young players. Thanks to the talented violinists who posed for the photos: Grennan Kim, Jeremy Black, Helen Choi, Hanna Mathey and Rachael Schoenberg. Our gratitude to all the past pedagogues who have contributed to current teaching concepts and to all present teachers who continue to develop and apply essential principles of teaching and enrich the educational, social and musical qualities in young students.

PREFACE

All string teachers must find an effective and efficient pedagogy to guide a student through the complexities of playing with accurate and tension-free left hand and bowing techniques. Knowing the proper order of developing technical and musical skills and knowing how to teach these essentials is necessary to bring excellent results. Positive outcomes are obtained when the teaching approach is well organized and properly sequenced.

The first step is to select an attractive repertoire that is sequential according to keys, range, rhythms, bowings, articulations, string crossings, form, etc. Each piece is selected to introduce new technical and musical ideas as well as repeating these from previous ones.

The next step is to find ways to work out any new techniques or problems in a piece by selecting related materials such as special exercises, mini-exercises, scales and etudes. Each piece contributes in a special way. Students not only solve the immediate difficulties in a piece, but with this intense study, gain solid techniques.

It is very important to teach the student to be a proficient "practicer." With this ability, the student is able to diagnose the problem of an awkward passage, how to practice to remedy it, and what type of exercise or related material to use to help solve it; also how to structure the general practice routine. The teaching and learning process has now reached its optimum level bringing quicker and more satisfactory results.

This text presents ways to organize an interesting and productive pedagogy that develops left hand and bowing techniques from beginning (Grade 1) through intermediate levels (Grade 5). Explanations and illustrations on each technical obstacle in the repertoire are analyzed and worked out to obtain fluent playing through the use of related material. Reviewing and refining earlier pieces leads to mastery and establishes an excellent playing foundation for new pieces.

The text is designed for both private studio and classroom string teachers.

OVERVIEW OF CONTENTS

CHAPTER 1: The Preparatory Period.

This section presents a step-by-step approach to teaching the basic bow hold and bowing movements for flexible and tension-free playing. It starts with simple strokes using scale patterns and short familiar songs executed with silent bowing motions (e.g. bowing over left shoulder). Meanwhile, playing posture, left hand position and finger patterns/placements are taught. Pizzicato is used to focus on proper finger placements (intonation) using the same scale patterns and songs. When each hand is functioning well, they are brought together. Special exercises working out each technique are included with explanations and illustrations. A Dalcroze eurhythmic program suggests ways to develop and internalize aural and rhythmic skills. These musical concepts are then applied to the scale patterns, preparatory songs and "Twinkle" rhythms. This interrelates the mental and physical aspects resulting in an effective way to teach and learn. The preparatory period develops technical and musical playing skills which serve as a prelude to the Suzuki Volume 1 repertoire. Listening to the Suzuki recordings while studying the pieces is encouraged. The student hears and absorbs the melody, tone quality, rhythm, articulations and musical form of this music that is to be learned.

CHAPTER 2: Exercises in Developing Control and Flexibility in the Bow Hold and in Bowing Movements.

Special bow hold exercises are introduced to help develop strength, control and flexible movements in fingers, wrist and arm. This includes teaching the physical motions when playing in each part of the bow, crossing strings, round bow motion (lift and reset) and refined finger and wrist action when changing bow strokes.

CHAPTER 3: Developing Left Hand and Finger Dexterity from Beginning Movements to Advanced Trills.

Exercises concentrate on proper finger action to perform tension-free, flexible movements. They start with simple quarter note exercises and work toward 16 slurred notes to a bow. An excellent preparation for playing perpetual motions and trills.

CHAPTER 4: Interrelating Repertoire with Mini-Exercises, Scales and Etudes.

As a student begins to work on a new piece, technical and musical problems may occur. These are extracted and studied separately, analyzed and practiced with simple mini-exercises and scales. At a more advanced level, etudes are also used to improve and strengthen techniques. The problems are worked out systematically. This not only improves the weak areas but adds to the general playing ability.

CHAPTER 5: The Scale: Building Techniques and Musical Skills.

This section presents ways to use the scale in the daily practice schedule when working out problems in the pieces. A problem indicates that a particular technique needs to be studied and strengthened. The diatonic scale is the least complex way to work these out. This chapter also demonstrates the many different technical and musical skills that can be achieved with the scale.

CHAPTER 6: Teaching Change of Position.

To prepare for this important and complex technique, a series of simple exercises can be started in Suzuki Volume 1 (e.g. "Allegretto"). These help to acquire the proper combination of physical movements for accurate and tension-free shifting. Also included are principles of proper shifting that can be applied to intermediate and advanced repertoire.

CHAPTER 7: Teaching the Vibrato from Beginning to Advanced Levels.

Preliminary vibrato exercises can be started in Suzuki Volume 1 (e.g. "Gavotte"). This chapter takes a student from the beginning stage to a fully developed vibrato and its application to repertoire.

CHAPTER 8: Bowing Articulations.

Definitions of bowing articulations with related markings are included. Explains how each is executed with application to musical examples.

CHAPTER 9: Teaching and Practicing.

Suggestions are presented in creating an approach to teaching, teaching students how to practice and a rote to note reading program. Also included: designing a daily practice schedule, pedagogical games to motivate students and social development activities.

CHAPTER 10: Playing Double Stops and Chords.

Presents ways to develop accurate interval relationships. Addresses special bowing techniques for producing a good tone quality playing double stops and 3-4 note chords.

CHAPTER 11: Private Studio and Classroom String Teaching Programs: Alternatives.

Teaching curriculums for the private and classroom string teachers are presented. A listing of repertoire (solo pieces) coordinated with the string method books and ensemble/orchestra music is enclosed. To develop note reading, a pre-reading program is included starting with eurhythmic activities which teach the musical concepts of rhythm, pitch and meter. This secures intonation and rhythmic playing as well as accelerates note reading. The string method book is often used to develop reading notes, rhythm, keys, positions, change of position, articulations, etc. **Quick Steps To Note Reading** is another source of teaching the essentials of note reading.

CHAPTER 12: Keeping Interest Alive (Motivating Students).

How to get an interesting start and teaching a student to become a productive "practicer." Also, making music with others using group instruction and ensemble playing.

CHAPTER 13: Learning Music Through Musical Form.

Defines and illustrates the structure of form (e.g. phrases, sentences). Examples of learning music using form from selected pieces in Volumes 1 and 2 of the Suzuki Violin School.

CHAPTER 14: Creating an Effective Pedagogy.

Identifies the contents of an interesting and productive teaching program. What is good teaching and how it is developed. Includes a description of various schools of pedagogy and how these can assist in constructing one's own approach to teaching.

RESOURCE A: The Dalcroze Influence on String Pedagogy
B: Pizzicato Playing
C: Chinrests, Shoulder Pads and Rests
D: Parts of the Violin and Bow
E: Glossary of Terms Used in text

REFERENCES

COMMENTS:

This text is basically an eclectic approach and applies teaching principles and concepts from renowned past and present pedagogues as well as personal teaching experiences. It relates how various instructional ideas can be studied and adapted to form an interesting pedagogy by utilizing a wide range of resources. How these are consolidated is discussed in Chapter 14: Creating an Effective Pedagogy. The ideas presented can be incorporated into any method or can serve as a complete method and teaching guide. It is designed for private studio and classroom string teachers.

The Suzuki repertoire is used in this text as an example of a well organized and interesting collection of pieces used to build technical and musical playing skills. Related general exercises, mini-exercises, scales and etudes assist in working out technical and musical problems in the pieces. Examples with explanations are presented from beginning through intermediate levels applying this interrelated material. Suzuki-trained students and students from other rote pedagogies may use this text but delay etude study until reading abilities have been achieved. However, mini-exercises, general exercises and scales can be used to develop techniques in pieces. These can all be taught by rote.

Short etudes are included while studying Suzuki Volume 1 pieces for those who are readers. The use of the etude and when it should be introduced is determined by the teacher. Etudes play an extremely important part in developing and strengthening techniques.

The Suzuki pieces in parentheses indicate when a particular exercise can be studied.

CHAPTER 1
THE PREPARATORY PERIOD

I.   INTRODUCTION: AN EXPLANATION OF THE FIRST STAGE OF DEVELOPMENT 10

II.   DEVELOPING BASIC BOWING MOVEMENTS 10

III.   PLAYING POSITION AND LEFT HAND POSITION 16

IV.   APPLYING BOWING ACTION ON OPEN STRINGS 20

V.   LEFT HAND POSITION AND FINGER PLACEMENT 21

VI.   INTRODUCING "PRE-TWINKLE" (PREPARATORY) SONGS AND SCALE PATTERNS ...24

VII.   BOW AND LEFT HAND TOGETHER 26

VIII.   RHYTHM NAMES TO "TWINKLE" VARIATIONS 34

IX.   OUTLINE: PREPARATORY PERIOD PRACTICE FORMAT. REVIEW OF CHAPTER 1 35

X.   HOW THE BOW ARM CAN AFFECT TONE QUALITY AND VOLUME 35

XI.   MUSICAL CONCEPTS LEARNED THROUGH DALCROZE EURHYTHMICS AND
        ITS INFLUENCE ON LEFT HAND AND BOWING TECHNIQUES 37

XII.   MUSICAL CONCEPTS AND REPERTOIRE LEARNED FROM
        THE SUZUKI RECORDINGS 40

CHAPTER 1
THE PREPARATORY PERIOD

I. INTRODUCTION: AN EXPLANATION OF THE FIRST STAGE OF DEVELOPMENT

The left hand and bowing techniques must function well individually before they can be brought together. Each hand operates differently, yet the two hands must be able to work together in order to deliver a satisfactory musical and technical performance. Learning to play the violin is an extremely complex activity. With this in mind, it is better to start with simple tasks and gradually add new techniques in proper order, working with hands separately. Each hand should be working correctly, be well controlled and free of tension. It may take several weeks before each hand reaches a correct and comfortable level. Only when this level is achieved should the left hand and bow hand be combined. The successful playing of repertoire can be attained more quickly and accurately with this approach than if the two hands are brought together from the very beginning.

A mental/physical relationship is essential in developing any type of complex skill. To achieve this, take a simple understandable task, practice it until it functions properly and then add the next step. The conscious and deliberate practice of this simple task repeated several times can bring it into an automatic response. If carefully studied and sequenced, a complex skill can be readily achieved with this step-by-step procedure.

It is recommended that the beginning stage also contain a pedagogy that develops musical learning and integrate it with skill development. Musical learning is defined here in terms of aural skills (ear training) and rhythm development which is used to guide the movement of left hand and bowing actions. A rote approach is used at this beginning level so that all the attention can be placed on integrating musical and technical skills. Simple and familiar songs with limited range and rhythms are used. Singing and walking (and/or clapping) and matching the notes and rhythms of the songs first before playing them on the instrument establishes the musical structure. Resource A explains how Dalcroze eurhythmic activities can be implemented. The physical/mechanical aspect follows with the ear helping to guide the fingers. Pizzicato playing is suggested at first to focus on left hand position and proper finger placement. A finger measurement system is highly recommended in this early period, that is, keeping fingers down whenever possible, especially when larger intervals are involved. Meanwhile, special attention is given to the bow hold and bowing action. Bowing these early songs over the left shoulder (silent bowing) integrates proper bowing action of wrist, hand and forearm with the rhythms of these songs. Each hand is mentally, musically and physically developed separately using the same repertoire. When each is functioning properly, the bow is placed on the string, with left hand and bow working together. Scale patterns are used to outline the range and rhythms of songs and to aid in coordinating left hand and bowing.

The foundation of all this technical and musical achievement is through a Dalcroze aural and rhythmic internal development program. Simple solo pieces, special exercises, mini-exercises and scale patterns are used in this early period to assist the young student in learning basic playing skills. The student is now prepared to proceed into Suzuki Volume 1 repertoire with left hand and bowing techniques working together in a very proficient manner with an excellent intrinsic development of aural and rhythmic qualities.

II. DEVELOPING BASIC BOWING MOVEMENTS

This section includes a detailed and sequential approach for developing beginning bowing techniques in the preparatory period. Early songs, exercises and related scale patterns are used to establish a flexible bow hold and proper bowing action.

A. Establishing Basic Bowing Action (Scratching the Left Forearm)

The middle of the bow is where most of the beginning Suzuki Volume 1 repertoire is played:"Twinkle," "Lightly Row," etc. These primarily consist of staccato and détaché bowings. Every bowing and articulation movement must be analyzed as to what parts of the bow arm are to be used. The basic movement is to come from the forearm and elbow playing at the middle part of the bow. This keeps the upper arm operating with minimum action and the shoulder free of any tight or stiff feeling. An interesting exercise to practice this initial movement is "scratching the arm."

In a sitting position, place the left hand on the left knee with a straight arm. With the right hand, form a bow hold and place it on the left forearm. Keep all fingers curved around the top of the arm and the thumb curved underneath opposite the second finger. All fingers are curved as if holding a ball. Keep right wrist, hand, forearm flat. Now bow ♩ ♩ ♩ ♩ ; the preparatory ("Pre-Twinkle") songs and "Twinkle" rhythms. Students can sing the melody with words while bowing to coordinate bowing action (rhythm) with melody (aural skills). Remember, the basic movement is that of the lower arm (forearm) and a flexible elbow working together.

In sitting position left hand on left knee with straight arm. Bow hand moving rhythms on left forearm.

B. Basic Bow Hold (Exercises to Achieve Control and Flexibility)
["Pre-Twinkle" Songs; "Twinkle" Variations]

Holding the bow is a new experience for the beginning student. However, it is absolutely essential that the proper formation be achieved in order to establish a flexible and well-controlled bowing action. In fact, the successful execution of all bowings depends upon a correct bow hold and its tension-free movements. Because the hold is so vital to good bowing action and because it is a complex technique, a systematic approach to develop this is recommended.

All fingers must be curved. This helps to control the bow and provides flexibility. Try an exercise to practice curving the fingers of a bow hold: "Close Hand, Open Hand." Make a fist, then open right hand (second finger and thumb opposite each other).

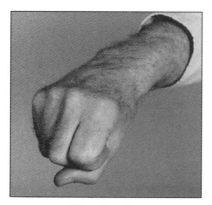

Close hand.

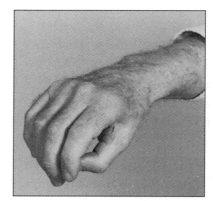

Open hand. All fingers curved.

Make a circle "O" with right hand with tip of thumb touching the top joint of the second finger.

Notice the curved thumb.

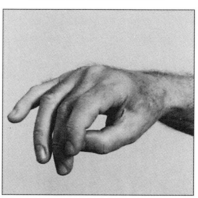

C. Practice Bow Hold on Pencil, then Transfer to Bow

Step 1: With a pen, draw a mark on the side of first finger between the first and second joint. Place a Dr. Scholl's corn pad on the pencil at the spot where the tip of the fourth finger should be. Place first finger on the mark and fourth finger on the corn pad. The second and third fingers are placed over the pencil. The curved thumb is opposite the second finger.

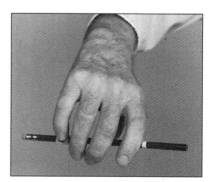

Bow hold on pencil with a pad.

Mark   Pad

Step 2: To develop strength, control and flexibility of fingers and wrist of the bow hold:
(a) With bow hold on pencil, hold arm horizontally about chest high in playing position. Move wrist/hand up and down (↕).
(b) Rotate hand while holding pencil (↶↷).

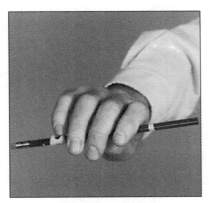

Pencil/bow hold.
(a) Up and down ↕

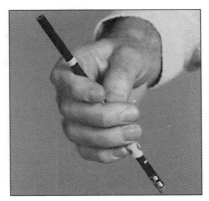

Pencil/bow hold.
(b) Rotate ↶↷

Step 3: Transfer bow hold from pencil to the real bow. Place tape on bow where the first finger should make contact. The pen mark on the first finger (between the first and second joint) helps to place the finger at its correct contact point. The fourth finger must be curved to give the fingers, hand and wrist mobility and control. The distance between the third and fourth fingers depends on the length of the fourth, but they must be curved at all times. The tip of the fourth finger rests on the corn pad which is positioned on the inner side of the octagon contacting the flat surface just next to the top on the player's side. This placement is important as it prevents the fourth finger from sliding off the stick as it assists in the articulation of various bowings and helps to balance the weight of the bow. The right corner of the thumb nail is placed where the bow stick meets the ebony (frog). Thumb pressure should be applied at an angle toward the frog and not at a right angle toward the stick. The thumb must also be curved at all times. The second and third fingers contact the bow near the first joints. The markers on the bow and first finger serve as visual guides to a nicely shaped bow hold.

The basic bow hold places the fingers about an equal distance from one another with the first finger slightly further away from the second. A properly balanced hold gives control, security and mobility to the bow as it plays through various articulations, in all parts of the bow, dynamics, tempos and when changing strings. If fingers are placed too close together, they lack control and if weight is added to produce a louder sound, a harsh tone results. If fingers are placed too far apart, flexibility is lost in the entire hand.

Bow hold.

Step 4: Place the middle of the bow on the left shoulder. Notice the "square" in the arm. The forearm is at a right angle to the upper arm. The wrist and forearm are almost flat.

"Square" in arm.

D. The Responsibility of Each Finger of the Bow Hold

First: This finger can supply additional weight (from arm) into the bow for an increase in volume, especially when playing at the upper part of the bow. It adds and releases weight required for accents, staccato and martelé playing. It provides flexibility and control when changing bow strokes. However, excessive weight when playing at the middle or lower part of the bow can cause an unpleasant tone quality.

Second, third and thumb: When additional volume is required, weight from the arm goes into the middle fingers (second, third) and thumb which form the center of the bow hold. These work together with the fourth finger when controlling tone quality and volume from the middle to lower part of the bow. The second and third fingers and thumb have an extremely important role in maintaining balance in the bow hold. To help develop bow balance, strength and control of the second and third fingers and thumb, practice exercises such as staccato and détaché strokes on open strings and scale patterns (♩ ♩ ♩ ♩ | ♫ ♫ ♫ ♫) in middle part of the bow with first and fourth fingers off the stick.

Fourth: The first and fourth fingers do give support to the second and third fingers when playing at the middle. The fourth finger is very important when playing at the lower part of the frog by assisting in controlling bow movements. The "push and pull" hand and finger motion used when changing strokes requires flexible movements from all fingers and the wrist. It is recommended that the fourth finger be kept on the bow when performing all bowings with the exception of tremolo.

It is extremely important to teach students from the very beginning the correct placement and function of each finger of the bow hold. Chapter 2 contains exercises for developing strength, control and mobility of the bow hold and hand and explains how these coordinate with other parts of the arm to produce an excellent bowing technique.

E. Suzuki Beginning Bow Hold

Two principles create an effective bow hold: (1) all fingers and thumb are curved for flexibility of movement; (2) the curved thumb is positioned opposite the middle fingers to maintain balance and control. It may be difficult to sustain a curved thumb in its regular position in this early stage and beginning students often develop one that is straight and inflexible.

Suzuki suggests that the thumb be placed initially on the outside of the frog. The corner of the curved thumb is positioned so it touches "Half on the silver (ferrule) and half on the hair." Notice that the thumb in this position is centered in the middle of the hand opposite the middle fingers creating an excellent balance. It is also placed where it can be moved into its regular position on the bow stick without realignment of finger or thumb angles. All fingers are nicely curved.

Suzuki's **Tonalization** exercises strive for a resonant sound on each tone when playing at different parts of the bow, different rhythms and articulations and at various dynamic levels. Weight adjustment of the arm into the middle fingers and thumb ("Thumb Power") assists in playing loud and soft dynamics. The beginning bowing is the staccato played at the center of the bow. The flexible forearm/elbow movement on each note eliminates tension in the upper arm and shoulder and helps to produce a resonant tone quality. This movement is essential whether playing at the middle or top of the bow. All this is studied and developed with the very mobile curved fingers and thumb. Achieving a good tone quality is an important objective in Suzuki's teaching and it starts at the beginning level.

When the student's hold is stable and the basic bowing actions are achieved, the thumb can be moved to its regular position with little incident. (It should be noted that the outside thumb position is reported to have been used by violinists before Suzuki as a relaxing change during the learning of new repertoire.)

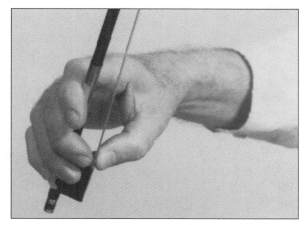
Suzuki bow hold. Thumb under frog.

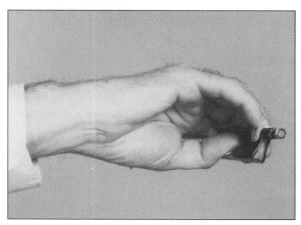
Thumb in regular position.

F.   "Silent Bowing": Practicing Bowing Movements with Rhythms and Songs ["Pre-Twinkle" Songs, "Twinkle"]

Place the middle of the bow on the left shoulder. Now that the hold is established, the next step is to develop proper bowing action. It is suggested that the first rhythms and songs be played between the two middle markers. This places the bow arm in a well-balanced playing position. A square in the bow arm is formed. The basic action is a forearm movement initiated by the elbow, with the upper arm and shoulder quiet and tension-free.

Exercise 1 (Bowing Over Left Shoulder). Bow staccato quarter notes (music) between the middle markers. At this early stage, staccato playing is described by Suzuki as "Legato Playing with Stops," but played with a firm tone quality. The staccato articulation is a complex action of weight ("bite") into middle fingers, a quick release and a quick, firm draw, then a stop. For the beginning student, however, producing a stiff staccato stroke can create a harsh tone and a tight bow arm. Therefore, it is advisable to modify this to "Legato playing with stops." Usually the refinement of real staccato playing can be developed by "Perpetual Motion" when basic bowing movements have been refined.

Practice (♩ ♩ ♩ ♩ ‖) to be played

♪ ⁊ ♪ ⁊ ♪ ⁊ ♪ ⁊ ‖

Bowing through a cardboard tube can be used to help control this silent bowing exercise.

Silent bowing through tube.[1]

Exercise 2 (Preparatory Songs). Students can sing songs while silent bowing rhythms. Singing early repertoire on pitch develops a good aural skill foundation and relates it to the rhythm of the notes played by the bow arm. The songs are listed at the end of Chapter 1.

MARY HAD A LITTLE LAMB

Sing: Ma-ry had a   lit-tle lamb,   lit-tle lamb,   lit-tle lamb.

Bow:

Exercise 3 (Continue silent bowing on "Twinkle" and rhythms).

After bowing these quarter note songs and obtaining proper bowing action, "Twinkle" and variations (rhythms) can be introduced. While the bowing arm is being developed with these rhythms and repertoire, the left hand is using the pizzicato approach to focus on the left hand position and proper fingering. In other words, the student is developing each hand while working on the same repertoire. When each is functioning well, putting them together will bring better results, rather than trying to coordinate both hands from the beginning.

III. PLAYING POSITION AND LEFT HAND POSITION
A. Rest Positions

It is important to establish a proper rest position first which will assist in obtaining a correct and balanced playing position. There are two kinds of rest positions: (1) when standing for lessons, practice, and other standing activities; (2) when sitting (usually for ensemble and orchestra playing).

1. **Standing:** Place violin under right arm so the upper arm covers the tail piece and the bridge remains visible. Keep scroll slightly elevated with bow pointing toward floor. Body is erect and feet are "V" shape.

2. **Sitting:** Place violin upright on left knee with bow across legs. Feet are "V" shape. Body is erect without touching back of chair. Or, place violin under right arm similar to the standing position.

B. Playing Position (Standing)

1. Place feet with heels together and toes pointing outward in a "V" position.

2. Move the right foot back so that the heels are about 6 to 8 inches apart. The feet are about the same width as the shoulders. This position creates an excellent body and playing balance. When playing, however, more weight is placed on the left foot (playing "into the violin").

3. The body should not be rigid. It should be flexible, tension-free and balanced. A good exercise is to transfer weight from one foot to another (rocking back and forth and bending the knees slightly).

1. Standing position of feet.
2. Playing position.
3. Balance weight on both feet.

C. Body Posture: "Walking the Violin"[2]

An activity to obtain an erect posture and release any body tension is "Walking the Violin." The violin is held above the head with both hands. While walking in time, sing the "Pre-Twinkle" songs and "Twinkle" with Variations. The teacher can play these pieces on the violin or piano. This aural and rhythm exercise helps to ease tension and keeps the body mobile and upright. It also prepares the repertoire the student will soon play. It develops and coordinates the musical proficiency of pitch, rhythm and meter which is directly applied to the pieces.

Walking the Violin.

D. Forming the Left Hand Playing Position

Three different approaches are listed:

1. Now that the standing posture has been learned, grasp the violin at the right bout with the left hand and place it under the chin in playing position. The head turns to the left without tilting (erect) and the back bout of the violin is placed well up on the shoulder (collar bone), virtually to the back edge of the shoulder. The tail button points into the neck. The shoulder is in normal position and should not be raised to meet the violin. This would cause tension in the left arm and affect mobility. A chinrest with a slight ridge over the tailpiece together with an appropriate shoulder pad will help support and balance the instrument. The violin is held parallel to the floor and the nose and face point down the fingerboard. It should be angled slightly downward on the right side to facilitate bowing on all the strings.

Correct stance and playing position.

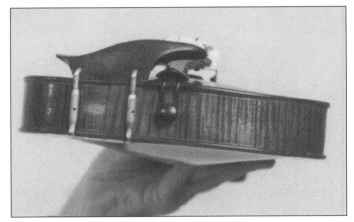

Slight ridge over tailpiece.

It is extremely important that each student be fitted with the proper size and height chinrest and shoulder pad to avoid a clutching effect between the chin and shoulder (collar bone). Resource C discusses types and sizes of chinrests, shoulder rests and pads.

18

2. Another approach to positioning the violin is to place the left hand on the right shoulder. This brings the left hand to playing level and the left elbow to playing position. Next, move hand out to playing position at the same level as the shoulder. Elbow is above the left knee and toes. Turn head to left facing the hand. Place violin in a "V" shape frame formed by the upper arm, forearm and wrist.

Left hand on right shoulder.

Violin in place.

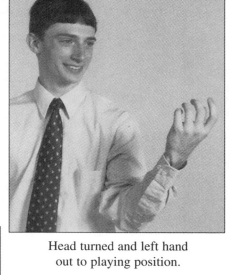

Head turned and left hand out to playing position.

3. The "Aim Toward Sky" game can be used to establish a proper playing position:

(a) In a standing, playing position (right foot back at about a 45° angle and equal to the width of the shoulder), hold the violin on the right side of the bout and swing it over left foot toward "sky" with a completely extended arm. Turn head to left to view back of violin.

(b) Bring instrument into playing position. Line-up: "Nose, elbow, knee, toes." The chin pulls the chinrest down and back toward neck. The shoulder should not push upward. If there is a space between the collarbone and the violin, fill it in with a proper height chinrest and shoulder pad. The violin should be slightly slanted to the right.

c) Drop both arms to the side of the body. The violin should be held in place with support from the collarbone and the weight of the head. Relax arms to release tension in shoulder and arms and to check if the chinrest and shoulder pad have been properly selected to keep the shoulder in its normal position.

IV. APPLYING BOWING ACTION ON OPEN STRINGS

A short staccato stroke played in the middle part of the bow is the first bowing presented to the beginning student. This bow stroke produces a firm, clear tone. A small amount of bow is used with stops after every note which gives the student time to prepare for the next stroke and time to set the next finger. Section IIC explains staccato playing and its initial development with silent bowing exercises.

Place an orange marking on the string or a tape on the instrument under the strings indicating the path of the bow. This photo shows the four left-hand finger placement markers and the bow guide marker.

Violin with four finger markers and marker for path of bow.

The bow is placed on the A string at the middle. The staccato is produced by a forearm movement initiated by the elbow. If the student has difficulty achieving a flexible elbow motion, the teacher can hold the upper arm while the student learns to produce a forearm and elbow movement. This is a very important bowing action not only for this beginning staccato stroke, but a basic movement for the many different types of bowings that will follow. At home, the student can place the upper part of the arm against a wall. Check to see if there is a square in the bow arm. Now bow down and up using a staccato stroke. The wall keeps the upper arm motionless so that the forearm can move freely. When this bowing action is moving properly, step away from the wall and practice this flexible forearm, elbow movement. However, some upper arm will be involved but only secondary to this active forearm, elbow.

When this bowing movement is functioning well and producing a clear, firm tone quality with quarter notes, try the following "Twinkle" Variations applying this forearm, elbow movement:

Correct playing movements in this early period prevent any physical problem from developing.

V. LEFT HAND POSITION AND FINGER PLACEMENT

A. Left Hand Position:

Move left arm into playing position over left foot without violin. The upper arm and forearm form a right angle. Point all fingers toward ceiling with fingers, wrist and forearm in a straight line with a "V" shape between thumb and first finger. With a felt pen, draw a line just above the palm joint of the first finger.

Place violin in playing position (with right hand) into the "V" shape of the left hand. The marked first finger is placed against the nut of the fingerboard. With the first finger on the string, locate the thumb opposite this finger. If the hand is small, the thumb can be placed slightly forward of the first so the third and fourth fingers can function more easily. It should not have a tight grip on the neck but be supportive and flexible. The placement of the thumb depends on the size of the hand and should be in a comfortable position. If positioned too far back, a cramped thumb muscle will occur; if positioned too far forward, there will be excessive tension in the palm of the hand.

Keep all fingers pointing toward ceiling with fingers, wrist and forearm in a straight line over knee and toes. The marker places the hand in the proper playing position.

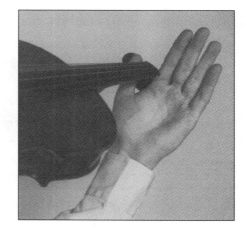

B. Markers on the Fingerboard:

These guides shape the hand and train the fingers/ear for proper intonation (spacing). This gives security in finger placement to the beginning student. Very thinly cut (1/16 inch) vinyl tape (available in rolls 1-1/2 inches wide) is placed on the fingerboard for positioning the four fingers. Place them on markers on A string (B - C# - D). If it does not disturb the hand position, place fourth finger on E string (pitch is B). Keep the first finger in contact with the nut to maintain a stable and secure hand. All fingers must be curved. Now move the fourth finger to the A string (pitch is E). If it is difficult to place the fourth finger properly (that is, nicely curved), delay using it until the other fingers and hand are comfortable and function properly.

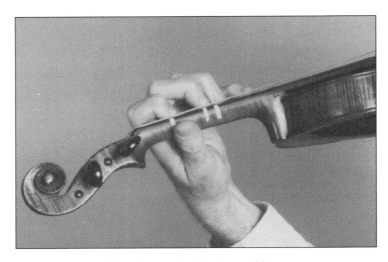

Four fingers in playing position.

C. The Following Exercises Develop Finger Dexterity.

Keep the hand quiet with fingers falling from base of knuckles onto markers. All fingers must be curved and tension-free. Do not pluck or bow, but use silent exercises to practice proper finger movements. These will also establish a foundation for correct finger spacing in the key of A major which is the key of the beginning songs and the first nine pieces in Volume 1 of the Suzuki Violin School.

First, line up the four fingers on the A string and then proceed to work on the dexterity exercises.

1. As a beginning exercise, keep first finger down instead of starting with the open string. This stabilizes the hand position. Move fingers up and down on markers with energy.

2. If a student is capable and it does not disturb the hand position, add the fourth finger.

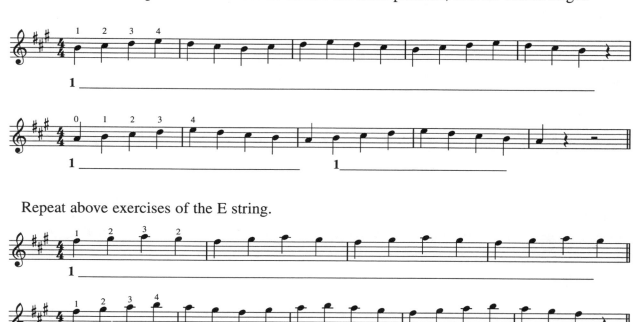

Repeat above exercises of the E string.

VI. INTRODUCING "PRE-TWINKLE" SONGS AND SCALE PATTERNS (KEY OF A MAJOR)

A. Pizzicato Scale Patterns. Use these patterns to concentrate on proper finger action and placement (intonation). This establishes the range of the songs. Refer to Resource B which explains pizzicato playing.

B. Pizzicato Songs.

Sing along while playing pizzicato which coordinates ear and finger placement. Transpose to E string.

MARY HAD A LITTLE LAMB

HOT CROSS BUNS

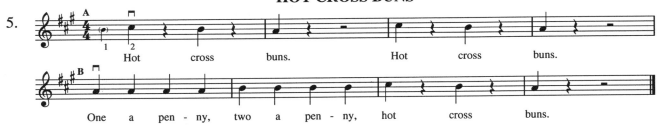

24

PIERROT'S DOOR

6.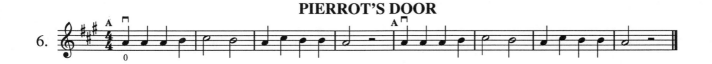

AUNT RHODY

7.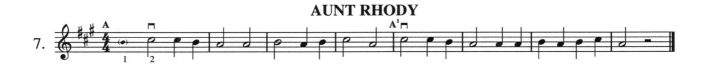

C. Next Use Silent Bowing (on Left Shoulder). This will help to focus on proper bowing movements while bowing and singing these "Pre-Twinkle" songs. This coordinates bowing rhythms with the melody (pitch). Use short staccato strokes on each note. The amount of bow is the same on all notes but a longer stop after the ♩ note.

Note: Because of the sensitive fingers of very young students (ages 4-9), it is suggested that one scale pattern (#1) and songs (#4-5) be practiced for several days. Then repeat scale pattern (#1) and proceed to songs (#6-7). Strive for a clear tone quality when plucking. Singing while plucking the song is an optional activity, but strongly encouraged. The purpose for doing both at the same time is to relate the inner ear (melody, pitch) to the pizzicato playing (rhythm). After the scale pattern and songs are secure on the A string, do them on the E string. Older students may progress through these exercises at a much faster rate. The objectives in this activity are to concentrate on the left hand position, finger patterns and relationships in this key, proper finger movements, ear training and playing basic rhythms. This is an excellent prerequisite to the pieces in Volume 1 (Suzuki) and similar repertoire.

D. Words to "Pre-Twinkle" (Preparatory) Songs:

4. Mary had a little lamb,
   Little lamb, little lamb
   Mary had a little lamb
   Its fleece was white as snow.

5. Hot Cross Buns.
   Hot Cross Buns.
   One a penny,
   Two a penny,
   Hot Cross Buns.

6. Pierrot's door is open,
   Open all the time.
   He is playing violin,
   Violin all the time.

7. Go tell Aunt Rhody,
   Go tell Aunt Rhody,
   Go tell Aunt Rhody
   Her old grey goose is dead.

8. See-Saw, See-Saw,
   This is the way we
   play See-Saw.
   See-Saw, See-Saw,
   This is the way we
   play See-Saw.

VII. BOW AND LEFT HAND TOGETHER (Using Preparatory Scales/Pieces, "Twinkle" Variations)

Now that the left hand, fingers and basic bowing movements are functioning well individually (using the same scale patterns and pieces), the hands are ready to be brought together.

The following are some of the goals to achieve in this next stage of development: solidify the left hand position, intonation (proper placement and spacing of fingers), flexible finger action, bow hold, bowing action and articulation, tone quality, correct bow placement and weight on strings, smooth bow changes, proper string crossing and clean coordination between fingers and bow. When these techniques have been carefully studied in this preparatory period, it is easy to see why this early period is so important in creating a good playing foundation.

The markers have been placed on the fingerboard to indicate accurate placement and spacing of the four fingers in the key of A major. The bow has two markers in the middle section where all the early songs and "Twinkle" rhythms are to be played. These markers ("helpers") guide the left hand fingers, and the bow movements correctly from the very beginning. As the student advances and security develops, the markers are removed.

A. Two Four-note Scale Patterns.

Staccato bowing is played with an equal amount of bow for each note, with good tone quality and bowing movements of the forearm which is initiated by the elbow joint.

This is to be played in the middle part of the bow. The stop after each staccato stroke allows time to make a clean finger change by placing the finger down before moving the bow.

Option: Play these scale patterns détaché ♩ ♩ ♩ ♩ ‖. Use the middle of the bow and strive for a smooth, even tone quality on each note.

B. Combine Scale Patterns

Do this on A and E strings creating an octave scale.

Lower the bow arm when crossing strings when ascending, and the hand will follow the arm. Raise the hand first when descending, and the arm will follow the hand. Raising the hand and arm together at the same level will cause excessive height and tension in the upper arm. Option: Also practice scale with détaché bowing.

C. Play Preparatory Songs

First play on A string with staccato bowing. Then transfer to the E string.

MARY HAD A LITTLE LAMB

HOT CROSS BUNS

Option: Also, play these songs with détaché bowing.

D. "See-Saw." Introducing a practice format using the scale and mini-exercises.

This is the first two-string piece containing a string crossing. It is an excellent preparation for the two-string "Twinkle" Variations. This introduces a practice format using the scale and mini-exercise to study problems and techniques in the piece. Continue staccato bowing.

SEE-SAW

1. Scale study of bowings and rhythms from "See-Saw," key of A major. Staccato bowing.

(a)

(b)

(c)

Amount and speed of bow is the same on all notes but a longer stop after the 𝅗𝅥. note. Keep strict time.

2. Mini-Exercises are used to work out problems in the piece. Concentrating on these problem areas and techniques in this piece will also prepare when they occur in future pieces.

(a) String crossing practice: first, rock bow between E and A strings at middle (silently); then play staccato notes stopping the bow stroke before changing strings. General principles: lower arm when ascending to next string and hand follows; raise hand when descending and arm will follow at a slightly lower level. Finally, play without stops and apply these string crossing movements.

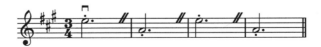

(b) Studying rhythm outline of piece on open strings.

28

First, play the ♩ and ♩. notes with the same amount and speed of bow but a longer stop after the longer note (♩.). Both of these rhythms receive the same staccato stroke as practiced on the scale (Section D #c). Then try to proportion the amount of bow with the rhythm; that is, the ♩ note receiving a shorter stroke than the ♩. note. Concentrate on even tone quality on all notes. Also, apply principles of string crossing.

For an early and enjoyable ensemble experience, use second and third parts and/or a piano accompaniment included in this chapter.

When qualified in détaché playing, study "See-Saw" with détaché and legato bowings.

MARY HAD A LITTLE LAMB

Piano Accompaniments

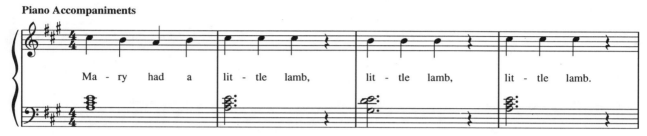

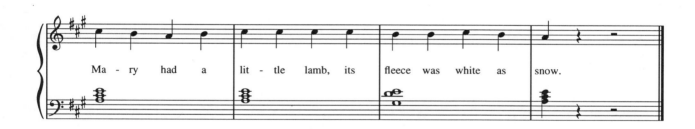

HOT CROSS BUNS

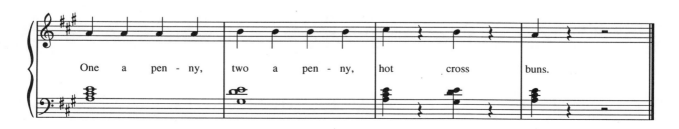

PIERROT'S DOOR

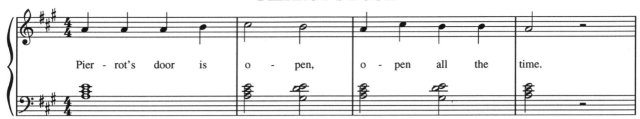

Pier - rot's door is o - pen, o - pen all the time.

He is play - ing vio - lin, vio - lin all the time.

GO TELL AUNT RHODY

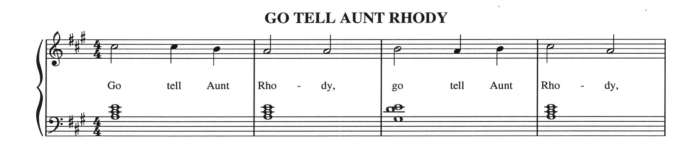

Go tell Aunt Rho - dy, go tell Aunt Rho - dy,

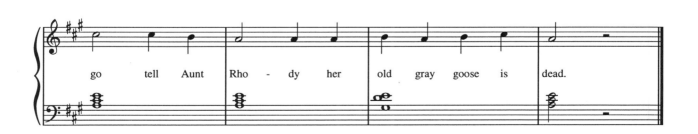

go tell Aunt Rho - dy her old gray goose is dead.

SEE-SAW

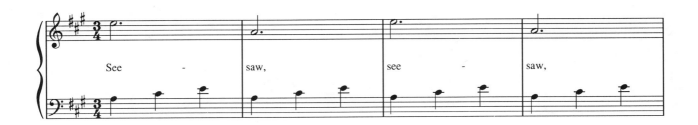

See - saw, see - saw,

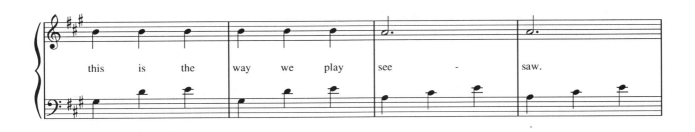

this is the way we play see - saw.

See - saw, see - saw,

this is the way we play see - saw.

MARY HAD A LITTLE LAMB

HOT CROSS BUNS

PIERROT'S DOOR

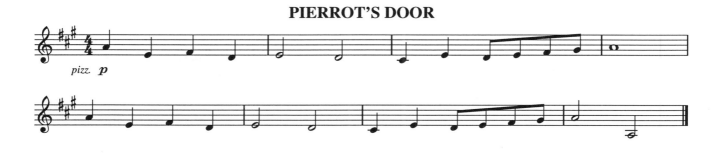

SEE-SAW

MARY HAD A LITTLE LAMB

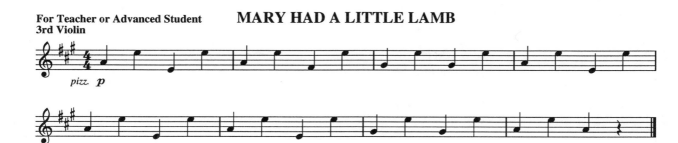

HOT CROSS BUNS

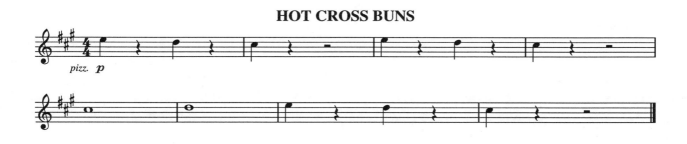

PIERROT'S DOOR

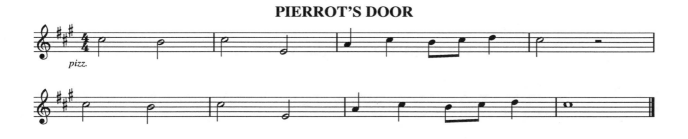

GO TELL AUNT RHODY

SEE-SAW

VIII. RHYTHM NAMES TO "TWINKLE" VARIATIONS

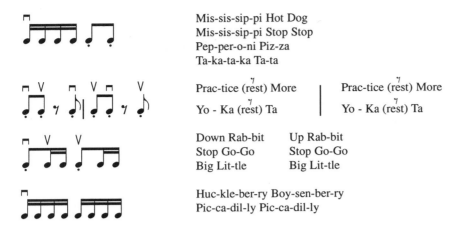

Mis-sis-sip-pi Hot Dog
Mis-sis-sip-pi Stop Stop
Pep-per-o-ni Piz-za
Ta-ka-ta-ka Ta-ta

Prac-tice (rest) More | Prac-tice (rest) More
Yo - Ka (rest) Ta | Yo - Ka (rest) Ta

Down Rab-bit   Up Rab-bit
Stop Go-Go   Stop Go-Go
Big Lit-tle   Big Lit-tle

Huc-kle-ber-ry Boy-sen-ber-ry
Pic-ca-dil-ly Pic-ca-dil-ly

Practice these rhythms using silent bowing over the left shoulder at middle of bow. Use a forearm movement which starts at the elbow. Say the words while bowing the rhythm. This develops and coordinates the inner senses of rhythm and melody with the physical movement of the bow arm. Use the same amount of bow for détaché and staccato bowings.

These basic rhythm and bowing variations appear often in repertoire. They not only develop proper bowing actions for the early pieces, but establish the playing proficiencies that appear in future pieces. For instance:

ALLEGRETTO (Volume 1 - Suzuki)

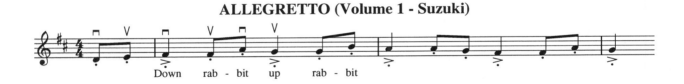

ANDANTINO (Volume 1 - Suzuki)

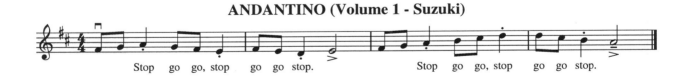

CONCERTO IN A MINOR - 1st MOVT. (Volume 4 - Vivaldi)

IX. OUTLINE: PREPARATORY PERIOD PRACTICE FORMAT. REVIEW OF CHAPTER 1

The preparatory period establishes a proper posture, left hand and bowing techniques; also, internal aural and rhythmic concepts. Simple tasks which are easy to learn build a foundation for more complex tasks. Techniques are learned separately and gradually integrated. The outline suggests how a practice format may be designed explaining how each skill is developed in the left hand and bow arm and when they are brought together. Details are in Chapter 1 (The Preparatory Period). This playing foundation prepares a student for regular repertoire such as Suzuki Volume 1.

Left Hand Development
1. Playing posture with violin.
2. Simple dexterity exercises: A/E strings. Use of markers to indicate finger placement and spacing.
3. Left hand played pizzicato (0-1-2-3-4). Use markers on fingerboard or orange marks on string. (Refer to resource B pizzicato playing.)
 * A-B-C#-D-E (0-1-2-3-4) A string
 * E-F#-G#-A-B (0-1-2-3-4) E string
 * Combine for an A major scale (♩;♩)
4. Dexterity exercises develop left hand and finger position and flexibility.
5. Pizzicato "pre-Twinkle" songs ("Mary Had a Little Lamb," etc.; also, "Twinkle" variations).

Bowing Techniques
1. Practice bow hold with pencil ("Teeter Totter," "Windshield Wiper") for control and flexibility.
2. Scratch left forearm with bow hold of right hand. Maintain flat wrist. Bowing action is primarily a forearm movement initiated by elbow.
3. Form bow hold. Silent bowing over left shoulder at middle of bow:
 ♩ ♩ ♩ ♩ short staccato strokes.
 "Pre-Twinkle" songs; "Twinkle" variations (sing while bowing to integrate pitch and rhythm).
4. Play rhythm of songs and "Twinkle" variations on A and E strings.
5. Tension-free exercises to develop strength, control, flexibility in bow arm.

When each hand is functioning well, coordinate them.
1. Start with scale patterns: A-B-C#-D-E; then E-F#-G#-A-B; then the A major scale. Use simple staccato strokes ♩ ♩ ♩ ♩ to each note. Progress to ♩ ♩ to each note. Also détaché.
2. Play "Twinkle" variations on scale patterns.
3. Play "pre-Twinkle" songs on A and E strings.
4. Continue to review and refine the left hand development and bowing technique exercises.

X. HOW THE BOW ARM CAN AFFECT TONE QUALITY AND VOLUME
A. The Bow Arm Can Affect Tone Quality and Volume in Various Ways:

(1) by the amount of weight placed into the bow; (2) increasing or decreasing the speed of the bow; (3) placing the bow in different positions between the fingerboard and bridge; (4) keeping the bow arm, wrist and fingers flexible so that the bow is drawn parallel to the bridge.

1. Controlling tone quality and volume is accomplished by adjusting the bow weight into the strings. When increasing volume at middle, the weight comes from the arm into the middle fingers and thumb with the shoulder and upper arm free of any excessive tightness or tension. Conversely, when decreasing the volume, release the arm weight. To create an even, sustained tone throughout a long

legato stroke, an increase in weight and flatter hair contact when approaching the tip will help maintain a consistent volume throughout the length of the bow. When playing at the tip, which is the highest part of the bow, the primary arm weight is placed into the first and second fingers of the bow hold.

2. Generally speaking, if there is an increase in the speed of the bow there will be an increase in volume. For instance, the short brisk staccato is the first bowing and articulation used in "pre-Twinkle," "Twinkle" and variations, and the initial stroke in "Lightly Row." These are played in the middle part of the bow for the beginning student. By placing a little more weight into the bow, a clearer, firmer tone is produced. Each stroke should be executed in the same way so that all notes are equal in sound and quality. Notice the square formed between the upper arm, forearm, bow and strings. The stop after each staccato note enables the beginning student to think of setting the next note. This is an excellent stroke and a good tone quality builder.

3. Tone quality and volume can also be controlled by the position of the bow on the string between the fingerboard and the bridge. Playing closer to the bridge will produce a more vibrant, louder tone, and conversely, playing nearer the fingerboard will create softer sounds. A little higher wrist will tilt the stick toward the fingerboard placing less weight with less hair contact on the string. This results in a lighter and softer sound. A flatter bow (with a flatter wrist position) and playing closer to the bridge will bring out a fuller, louder tone.

4. The bow should be drawn parallel to the bridge in a straight line. A crooked, slanted bow draw can influence tone quality as well as pitch. A narrow tape can be placed on the violin under the strings about halfway between the bridge and fingerboard to serve as a visual aid and assist the student in keeping the bow straight and bowing in the proper place. To create a straight bow stroke, the bow arm must be flexible, tension-free and well-coordinated with a combination of wrist, forearm and upper arm movements. Chapter 1 (The Preparatory Period) contains exercises to develop mobility in the various parts of the bow arm.

B. Position of Bow Arm When Playing at Different Parts of the Bow

1. Middle: The bow resting on the string at the middle shapes a square formed by the upper arm, forearm, bow and strings. Beginners start in the middle as this is the center of the bow where the bow arm movements are in the most flexible and comfortable position.

2. Frog: The arm is in a triangular position when playing at the frog. This shape is created by the upper arm, forearm, hand and violin. Weight on the bow for volume comes from the arm into the thumb and third and fourth fingers.

3. Top: When playing at the upper part of the bow, the arm is almost completely extended. A very slight bend in the elbow is necessary to keep the elbow joint mobile. Because this is the lightest part of the bow, more hair contact (a flatter bow) is used, and additional weight is transferred from the middle and fourth fingers to the first and second fingers. The wrist and hand move slightly down which helps to transfer this weight. All fingers are kept on the bow to maintain bow support and control.

Refer to exercises in Chapter 2 (Sections IV, V, VII) in developing a flexible and controlled bow hold and in coordinating bow arm movements in all parts of the bow.

XI. MUSICAL CONCEPTS LEARNED THROUGH DALCROZE EURHYTHMICS AND ITS INFLUENCE ON LEFT HAND AND BOWING TECHNIQUES
(See Resource A for further Dalcroze information)

An important objective in this Preparatory Period is to build a foundation of musical concepts by internalizing a rhythmic and aural response to music. It is suggested that a Dalcroze type program be instituted prior to and during this beginning stage of instruction. Aural response (solfegé) awakens the sense of musical pitch, tonal relations and tone quality. It promotes the ability to listen, to hear, to remember (tonal memory), to respond. It develops and interrelates the mental and physical aspects of playing. Marching, stepping or clapping the beat (meter) while singing (pitch) the preparatory and the early pieces in Grade 1 (Suzuki, Volume 1) will prepare the young student to hear and feel these songs internally. They can also be stepped to loud dynamics or tiptoed lightly to soft dynamics. Tempos can be learned through slow, medium, fast singing and stepping; also, a study of phrasing, crescendos and decrescendos. Students become sensitive to express rhythm by responding physically. Rhythmic movement also helps to retain and move the melodic line. This activity begins to coordinate meter, rhythm, pitch, dynamics, tempos. In a short time, these musical concepts are internalized creating an immediate and accurate response when applying them to left hand (pitch) and bowing movements (rhythm).

The Dalcroze program can be used in different ways depending on the teacher's pedagogical approach, the age of the student and the kind of teaching environment (private studio or classroom instruction). Two different approaches are listed below as examples illustrating how this eurhythmic program can be implemented:

A. Comprehensive Approach

A comprehensive program extending 2-8 weeks can be exclusively devoted to developing rhythmic and aural skills. The preparatory and Grade 1 (Volume 1) pieces are used not only to build these concepts but also are the very pieces that will be applied to the instrument. This activity is especially enjoyable for very young children (ages 3-5). Although they look forward to playing the instrument, being active physically and musically in eurhythmic activities can be fun. Stepping to the meter and singing the words on pitch with piano accompaniment can be easily accomplished by a very young student. Extending the song by applying different dynamic levels, forms, accents, etc. can develop a very musical child. This is indeed an excellent pre-instrumental music training program. Example of eurhythmics applied to repertoire:

MARY HAD A LITTLE LAMB

HOT CROSS BUNS

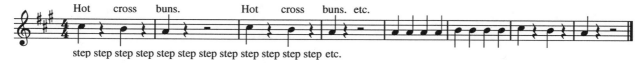

SEE-SAW

TWINKLE

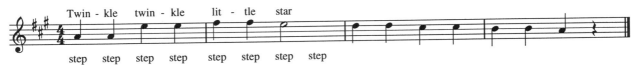

After completing this program, the young student is ready to learn the mechanics of playing the instrument with the help of this musical experience.

1. Application to left hand

While sitting with instrument in playing position, tap foot in time (meter) and pizzicato the notes. The student can call out the names of fingers while singing the notes (0-0-0-0; 1-1-1-1). Focus is on playing posture, left hand position, proper finger placement (use markers), rhythm and meter.

Start with a scale pattern to outline the range of the preparatory songs: Sing on pitch and pizzicato.

MARY HAD A LITTLE LAMB

If tapping the foot is difficult for the student while playing or it is not an approach selected by the teacher, clap meter while singing the notes on pitch before playing. It helps to outline the rhythm, meter and pitch.

Continue this scale and song relationship on the remaining preparatory songs and into the early pieces in Volume 1.

2. Application to bowing

Developing proper bowing movements is the next step. Silent bowing exercises over left shoulder include bowing the rhythm, singing songs on pitch and tapping the meter with the foot. This combines the internal musical concepts and applies them to the physical movement of the bow arm. The primary focus is to execute proper rhythm, articulation and bowing action in each song and coordinate them with the melodic line. This exercise can start with the preparatory songs and progress to "Twinkle" with Variations and into Volume 1 pieces. When progressing through this sequential repertoire, many different rhythms, articulations and bowing movements are being studied. This builds proper bowing actions in the beginning stage and prepares for subsequent pieces. Silent bowing practice coordinates rhythm, pitch, meter and proper bowing movements which in turn produces accurate intonation, good tone quality, proper articulations and bowing actions. The student is prepared for the next step — applying bowing on the instrument.

3. Play left hand and bow together using these early songs and "Twinkle" Variations.

B. A Modified Dalcroze Program

A shorter program can also be used to promote an internal musical foundation of rhythm, pitch and meter. For instance, older beginning students may want to play the instrument as soon as possible. However, both teacher and students should realize the importance of this eurhythmic training. Besides developing musical concepts, they learn how to apply these when approaching the instrument and music they soon will be playing. They realize how proficient their playing will be because of this experience. This program is applicable to both private studio and classroom instruction.

For instance, the period of time for this program can be limited to 2-3 weeks (3-5 sessions) before starting the instrument. Many intrinsic benefits can still be developed:

1. The primary focus would be on marching, clapping and singing the preparatory songs, "Twinkle" (and Variations) and some of the Volume 1 pieces, not only to develop these musical concepts, but to prepare the repertoire that will be played on the violin;

2. Next, tap the meter and play the rhythms of the piece on scale pizzicato;

3. Practice rhythms of piece with silent bowing while singing the melody;

4. Pluck the entire piece;

5. Final step, play left hand and bow together.

As a student progresses from the early preparatory songs into Volume 1 pieces, continue eurhythmic activities by marching, clapping and singing these tunes (review and refine). Augment activities to study tempos, dynamics and phrasing.

Note: These physical eurhythmic activities have another important function: They produce tension-free movements. The entire body responds and moves to rhythms and dynamics of the songs. This feeling is transferred into the bow arm. Although a specific group of joints and muscles are directly responsible for a particular bowing or articulation, adjacent ones are indirectly involved and supportive. Any restrictions create stiff motions. An immobile or a non-cooperative joint or muscle will prevent smooth actions. When bowing movements are studied with silent bowing on the early songs and "Twinkle" rhythms, the tension-free and coordinated arm movements can be easily observed and developed. The upper arm, elbow motion, forearm and wrist work together in various combinations depending on the rhythm, articulation, dynamic level and part of the bow being used. Mental involvement and control are essential in order to direct and guide a specific bowing movement. Daily repetition and refinement using this approach lead to a correctly executed and automatic bowing response. It is extremely important to obtain bowing techniques that are properly done in this beginning stage. It serves as a foundation for future intermediate and advanced bowings.

Another valuable outcome of this rhythm and aural skill development is that it contains the structure for note reading. This internal learning of musical concepts enables note reading to start earlier and to be conceived more quickly.

Conclusion: This concludes the Preparatory Period ("Pre-Twinkle"). The student is now ready for "Twinkle" (Variations) and other Volume 1 pieces. It is interesting to see how these early pieces can be interrelated with special exercises, scale patterns and bowings to create a foundation for good performing techniques and musicianship. All this is taught by rote in order to concentrate on the aural, rhythmic, technical and musical aspects of playing. If each step is made easy to understand and readily achievable, learning and motivation to practice will be at an optimal level.

XII. MUSICAL CONCEPTS AND REPERTOIRE LEARNED FROM THE SUZUKI RECORDINGS

The use of recordings of Suzuki repertoire for the young student is an excellent way to teach musical and technical concepts in the pieces. It develops internally the ability to transfer what is being heard to what is to be played. The ear absorbs and internalizes the melody, rhythm, articulation, dynamics, tempo, tone quality and form through repeated listening to a piece that is to be studied. Like developing a vocabulary through rote listening to simple words and sentences at an early age, the young violinist builds a musical "vocabulary" in the same way. The amazing ability to assimilate and imitate is an instinct that plays an important part in the educational process. Taking advantage of this natural instinct, Suzuki found a way to transfer and guide musical learning through model recordings. Of course, the primary source of development comes from the lessons with the teacher who utilizes the benefits of learning through listening.

Either the use of recordings or Dalcroze eurhythmics would benefit the musical growth of the young player. However, an interesting approach would be to combine these, with each contributing in its own special way. For example, during the Preparatory Period, the "pre-Twinkle" songs and early pieces in Volume 1 of the Suzuki Violin School can be used to develop aural and rhythmic skills internally with a Dalcroze program. While this is in progress, students can listen to the Suzuki recordings. With the Dalcroze singing and rhythm movements, and the listening to model recordings of the Volume 1 pieces, a combination of aural, rhythmic and musical concepts are internalized from two different but very compatible sources.

---

1. Paul Rolland, *Prelude in String Playing* (Boosey & Hawkes, New York, and Clara Rolland, Urbana, Illinois, 1971). Page 9.

2. Rolland, page 23.

CHAPTER 2
EXERCISES IN DEVELOPING CONTROL AND FLEXIBILITY IN THE BOW HOLD AND IN BOWING MOVEMENTS

I.   BOW HOLD AND BOW ARM EXERCISES ["TWINKLE," "LIGHTLY ROW"] 42

II.   DEVELOPING BOW ARM MOVEMENTS ["ALLEGRETTO"] 44

III. STRING CROSSINGS ["AUNT RHODY"]...46

IV.   DEVELOPING BOW HOLD AND BOW ARM MOVEMENTS WHEN PLAYING
      IN ALL PARTS OF THE BOW ["ALLEGRO"]...49

V.   PLAYING AT DIFFERENT PARTS OF THE BOW ["ALLEGRO"]..50

VI.   LIFT AND RESET MOTION [BOWINGS] (REPEATED DOWN BOW AND
      UP BOW STROKES) ["SONG OF THE WIND"]...52

VII. PLAYING IN ALL PARTS OF THE BOW AND REFINING BOW ARM
      MOVEMENTS ["ETUDE"]..53

CHAPTER 2
EXERCISES IN DEVELOPING CONTROL AND FLEXIBILITY IN THE BOW HOLD AND IN BOWING MOVEMENTS

I. BOW HOLD AND BOW ARM EXERCISES ["TWINKLE," "LIGHTLY ROW"]

The following exercises promote control, strength and flexibility in the bow hold and bow arm actions. Start when working on "Twinkle." All contain and encourage tension-free motions. These exercises will develop proper bowing movements for the early Volume 1 Suzuki pieces and will serve as a foundation for the more advanced music that follows. They are arranged in sequential order and progress at the same rate as the pieces. The exercises will help facilitate the techniques included in the piece and as the repertoire advances, the techniques advance.

Exercises:

1. Place the middle of the bow on the A string. Observe the square in the arm. Tap each finger of the bow hold.
2. Place bow on A string at the middle, press third and fourth fingers of the bow hold to raise the bow off the string (like a windshield wiper or turning a door knob).
3. Climbing the bow. Point bow toward ceiling with a regular bow hold. Climb bow stick with fingers keeping them curved as they travel upwards. Climb about one-half to two-thirds of bow and return to frog.
4. Form bow hold. Point bow, which is in front of body, toward ceiling. Move bow up (about eight inches) toward ceiling and return to original position. Keep bow arm and shoulder tension-free and flexible. This is called "The Rocket"—The bow going up and coming down.

4. Move bow toward ceiling and return. Keep shoulder joint flexible.

5. Point bow (which is in front of the body) toward ceiling and stir the pot (move bow in a circle). The bow arm and shoulder should be relaxed. Maintain a good bow hold with curved fingers.

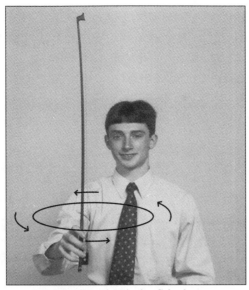

5. Move bow in circle. Stir the pot.

6. Point bow toward ceiling. With bow in front of the body, move bow back and forth horizontally (right to left; left to right). Keep shoulder joint relaxed and mobile. Do not rotate the upper body.

7. Hold bow parallel to the floor in front of the body at the playing level of the bow when placed on the violin. Move the bow up and down vertically (about eight to ten inches). Maintain a free arm and shoulder movement.

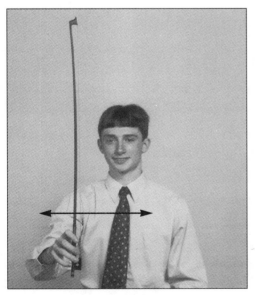

6. Move bow horizontally. ⟷

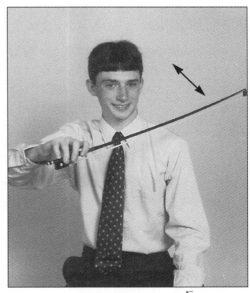

7. Move bow vertically. ↘

8. Keep all fingers curved in a normal bow hold position while doing this exercise. With bow held in playing position in front of body and parallel to floor, press fourth finger down making the bow point upward. Then press the first finger down returning bow to its original position (parallel to floor). The movement is similar to opening a door knob (semi-circular). At first, to keep the wrist and forearm in place and steady, hold the wrist with the left hand. After control is obtained, release the left hand support.

II. DEVELOPING BOW ARM MOVEMENTS ["ALLEGRETTO"]
A. Proper Weight Distribution Of Each Finger Of Bow Hold (Basic Exercise)

Place middle of bow on left shoulder to simulate the hand, forearm and upper arm playing position. Notice the square in the arm. Raise the first finger off the stick. The hand and forearm should almost be flat. The natural weight of the arm should progress into the middle fingers and thumb which is the center of the bow hold. Bow the "Twinkle" rhythms with a forward movement initiated by the elbow.

Now place the first finger lightly on the bow and repeat the rhythms. The first finger is being trained not to press into the bow but merely to aid in controlling the bowing action. Too much weight or pressure sustained throughout the note creates a harsh tone. The weight to produce a firm tone quality comes from the arm into the thumb and middle fingers. The first and fourth fingers do give support and balance to the bow hold when playing at the middle. The first finger, however, does place pressure into the bow, with a quick release, when articulating staccato, martelé, and accented notes, and when playing at the top of the bow. However, at the beginning stage, play the staccato, as Suzuki states, "Legato with a Stop."

B. Elbow Movement (When Playing In All Parts Of The Bow)

The elbow motion is the most neglected and underdeveloped part of the bow arm. The elbow is activated from the very beginning when working on the early exercises and pieces. It is involved when playing in all parts of the bow, and particularly in the middle and lower half. The preparatory songs and early Volume 1 pieces (e.g. "Twinkle," "Lightly Row," "Song of the Wind") are played at the middle of the bow where the forearm/elbow action is predominant.

It is also important to know that although this movement is initiated by the forearm and elbow, it is supported and coordinated by a tension-free motion in the upper arm and shoulder. This creates greater freedom of movement which will result in a smoother, more even tone quality. Any tight feeling or overuse of the upper arm is detrimental to tension-free bowing.

Any increase or decrease in volume should not be made by pressure from the wrist and fingers alone but by more or less weight from the arm into the wrist and middle fingers.

For a smooth bow change, there should be a slight circular movement in the wrist and fingers (⊓ V at frog) (V ⊓ at tip). Refer to Hand and Finger Section E for exercises to develop the finger/wrist bow change flexibility.

Exercises to promote coordination in the bow arm:
1. Place bow on left shoulder at the tip for an up-bow stroke. The hand, forearm and elbow move the bow toward the middle. As it reaches the middle, the square is formed. That is, the hand and forearm are almost flat — the forearm is at a right angle to the upper arm. As the hand, forearm and elbow move the bow toward the frog, the elbow becomes lower than the wrist and forearm. Keep the bow hold and wrist mobile with fingers curved and in control. Relax the shoulder.

When all parts of the bow arm are performing well, apply on open A string.

2. The down-bow stroke from the frog starts with the forearm and elbow moving the bow toward the middle and leads the way to the tip. Players find that this action by the forearm and elbow is similar to up-bow strokes, which continues moving the bow to the frog. The same motion applies when going down-bow. Elbow movement at the frog reduces the noise of the bow change at the frog. Keep the upper arm and shoulder free of any tight feeling. First practice with silent bowing then apply on open A string.

C. Forearm Movement

The forearm is involved in every bowing except tremolo and sautillé. For a short stroke or a longer stroke, the impulse comes from the forearm and elbow with some upper arm movement. The hand moves freely without any excessive tight feeling. Simulate this movement by pretending to bounce a ball. If these parts of the bow arm are not well coordinated, it will end up as a crooked bow stroke with a poor tone quality. When playing near the frog, there is some forearm motion and an increase in upper arm movement. Forearm action increases with upper arm movement when playing from middle to tip. In other words, forearm/upper arm movements always work together but in different ways depending on the part of the bow that is being used. Avoid any stiffness in the elbow or shoulder. Practice this action on "Twinkle" Variations at middle of bow. Also, practice in lower and upper part of bow. Apply exercises on A and D strings.

Détaché/staccato

D. Shoulder (Tension-Free)

The shoulder and shoulder joint should be without tension at all times to allow free forward and backward movement of the upper arm. The shoulder moves slightly up and down due to the elbow motion when playing in the lower half of the bow. It should not be raised or pushed into the neck at any time. For instance, to help hold the violin in place, an appropriate-fitting chinrest and shoulder pad can fill in the space between the collarbone and chin.

E. Hand And Fingers (Developing Flexibility)

Beginners playing the "Twinkle" rhythms are taught to move fingers, hand and forearm as one unit with action from the elbow. With the previous exercises (B, C), the finger and wrist joints become more flexible. However, while some students develop this agility easily, others may require additional finger and wrist exercises.

1. Hold a pencil with the normal bow hold (if needed, a Dr. Scholl's pad can help form a curved fourth finger). Move pencil as if playing up-bow and down-bow with fingers and hand with movement from wrist. The thumb must be curved and opposite the second finger to maintain bow hold balance. Keep the forearm quiet. A push (up-bow) and pull (down-bow) exercise.

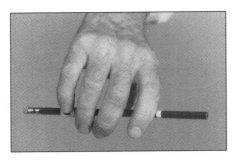

⊓ Pull (Down-Bow).

Push (Up-Bow).

2. Practice the above exercise with the bow on the A string at the middle. Push bow upward an inch or so with the fingers, hand and wrist without moving the forearm. Stop. Then pull down-bow with fingers, hand and wrist. Notice that the fingers are almost extended (fingers should still have some curve). Stop. Repeat up-bow push. The fingers, thumb, hand and wrist should bend with ease. When all moves well, repeat without stops creating a smooth bow change movement.

3. Hold a cardboard tube with the left hand in front of body at the same level as when playing the violin. Bow the following rhythms: 𝅝 | 𝅗𝅥 𝅗𝅥 ‖ 𝅗𝅥 𝅗𝅥 | 𝅗𝅥 𝅗𝅥 ‖ 𝅘𝅥 𝅘𝅥 𝅘𝅥 𝅘𝅥 ‖ and apply the pull and push technique when changing bow strokes. Notice that going up-bow, the fingers, hand and wrist are in a slightly upward position. Going down-bow, the flexible fingers, hand and wrist bend slightly. Raising the wrist too high when going up-bow or lowering it too much when playing down-bow results in less weight with less hair contact. This tilts the bow abnormally which destroys the smoothness and evenness of tone. The minimum raising and lowering together with a flexible finger, hand and wrist movement, when changing stokes will produce an even, smooth and continuous tone.

4. Apply 𝅝 | 𝅗𝅥 𝅗𝅥 ‖ 𝅗𝅥 𝅗𝅥 | 𝅗𝅥 𝅗𝅥 ‖ 𝅘𝅥 𝅘𝅥 𝅘𝅥 𝅘𝅥 ‖ with bow on A string.

Note: The above exercises are purposely exaggerated to develop this bowing technique. In actual playing, the fingers, hand and wrist move much less than in these exercises and very little in fast strokes. However, flexibility with proper execution should be available when changing bow strokes.

III. STRING CROSSINGS ("AUNT RHODY")

At the beginning stage, the entire arm is raised and lowered as a unit when changing strings. The shoulder, even at this early period, should be free of tightness or tension. As the student progresses, the movement is refined. General Rule: When crossing from a higher to a lower string, the hand leads and the elbow follows. When crossing to a higher string, the elbow drops first and the hand follows.

Exercises to develop proper string crossing movements:

A. "Roll the Bow"

With the violin in playing position, place bow at the middle on the E string. Roll over from E to G string and return to E. The hand and forearm move in an arc-like motion (‿⌐) across the strings. Apply the general rule when crossing strings.

"Roll the Bow"

From E to G string

and from G back to E

E String.

G String.

B. Crossing Two Strings

This string crossing principle applies to both separate and slurred notes. With violin in playing position place the bow at its middle on the A string. Roll the bow between two strings (e.g. A and D) with the natural weight of the arm and the hand leading the way. Now cross from D back to A with the elbow dropping first. Do the same between E/A - A/E; D/A - A/D; G/D - D/G. When this movement feels comfortable and is done correctly, play "Twinkle" rhythms between the two strings. For instance, play ♫♫♪ ♫♫♪ on the open A string. Stop. Cross from A to D. Play this same rhythm pattern on the open D. Stop. Cross from D up to the A string. Concentrate on crossing to next string with proper movements, then play. Gradually, eliminate stops. Apply on all strings: E/A; D/G.

C. String Crossing At The Frog

This should be made primarily with finger and wrist action in a semi-circular movement with some cooperative arm motion. Play at lower part of bow:

D. Crossing Three To Four Strings (Slurred Notes).

Adjust hand and elbow levels when going from string to string. Silent Exercise: Place bow at middle on G string. Notice that the wrist is above the elbow. Rock from G to E and from E to G. The elbow is lower on the G and the wrist higher. Going to the E string, the wrist is lowered so that it is about level with the elbow.

Practice with stops while crossing, then eliminate stops for smooth legato bow crossings. Use both down and up-bow approach.

Other string crossing exercises:

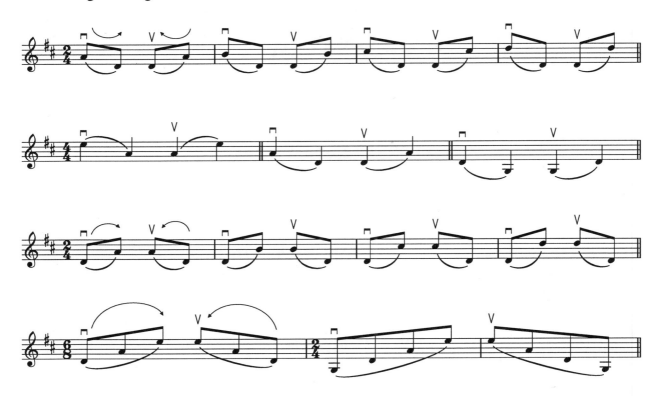

An interesting exercise is to play these at the top and lower part of the bow. Relax shoulder and keep it flexible. The bow arm must be under control when playing in all parts of the bow.

IV. DEVELOPING BOW HOLD AND BOW ARM MOVEMENTS WHEN PLAYING IN ALL PARTS OF THE BOW ["ALLEGRO"]

These exercises encourage a firm bow hold and help to control playing from the frog to tip.

Exercises:

A. Practice Bow-Control.

Place bow on A string at middle. Make sure that all fingers of bow hold are nicely curved and in control of the bow. Lift bow about six inches above strings, moving arm and bow as one unit—straight up. The wrist is higher than the elbow. Reset bow on the string smoothly. Keep shoulder relaxed.

B. Lift and Reset.[1]

Practice in all parts of the bow. Place bow on A string at middle. Observe square in arm and keep fingers nicely curved in the bow hold. Lift bow with an arc-like motion and place it on the string at the tip. Notice that the wrist is lower and the fingers are less curved than at the middle. Now lift bow and place it on the string at the frog. Notice that the wrist is higher than the elbow. This exercise enables the student to experience the position of the arm and shape of the fingers, hand and wrist at the different parts of the bow. It develops bow control by lifting and resetting the bow. Maintain a tension-free upper arm and shoulder.

At the Middle.   At the Tip.   At the Frog.

C. A Follow-Up Exercise To Above Part B

Lift and reset. Place bow on A string at middle and play ♩♩♩♩ (4 quarter notes). Lift bow and play at upper part. Lift bow and play at lower part of bow. Observe the proper bowing motion at each part of the bow. Repeat this exercise on other strings and adjust level of arm going from E to G and from G to E. The forearm and elbow initiate bowing movements when playing in all parts of the bow and on all strings.

V. PLAYING AT DIFFERENT PARTS OF THE BOW ["ALLEGRO"]

A. Divide the Bow Into Three Equal Parts (use markers). Play a four-measure quarter note exercise in each part of the bow. Then play the Preparatory songs in each part.

MARY HAD A LITTLE LAMB

Producing tone quality and volume in each part of the bow:

1. At lower part: This requires a forearm movement from the elbow with a flexible finger and wrist action when changing bows. The upper arm moves slightly forward and backward. Because this is the heavier part of the bow; less hair contact is used by slanting stick toward fingerboard.

2. At middle part: This is primarily a forearm movement initiated by the elbow. The bow arm opens and closes with hinge-like action. Weight is increased for a firmer tone and volume (if needed) from arm into forearm and into second, third fingers and thumb of the bow hold. Going into middle from the lower part, use more hair contact with bow only slightly slanted. Wrist and forearm are almost flat.

3. At upper part: There is less movement when playing in this part of the bow than at the middle, but more movement than at lower part. This is a forearm motion which starts at the elbow causing an in and out movement of the upper arm. The weight is increased coming from the arm into the first and second fingers of the bow hold with bow hair contact almost flat to equal the volume of the lower and middle sections; as this is the lightest part of the bow. Keep the fourth finger down to help balance and control the bow.

Exercise:

Experiment playing different dynamics: piano (*p*); forte (*f*). Besides weight adjustments and amount of hair contact, the position of the bow between the bridge and fingerboard is to be considered. Softer sounds are better produced when playing closer to the fingerboard, less weight into bow and less hair contact. Increase volume by playing closer to the bridge, more weight into bow and more hair (flatter bow). Practice on all strings creating equal tone quality and volume. Strive for a beautiful tone.

(a) Whole notes: ⊓̇o | ∨̇o with full bow (*p*, *f*)

(b) Quarter notes ♩ ♩ ♩ ♩ ‖ at lower, middle, upper third (*p*, *f*)

B. Playing At Different Parts Of The Bow On Different Strings

Two bowing principles are applied in the exercise:

1. Proper movements when playing at different parts of the bow as explained in section A (1-2-3). Play at middle, lower, upper part of bow.

2. Adjust bow arm levels when playing on different strings. When moving from lower to higher strings, the elbow drops first with the hand following. The hand leads the way going from upper to lower strings.

C. Obtaining A Sustained Legato Tone Quality Throughout The Bow

Divide the bow (use markers) and play slurred, sustained notes with a stop between each one. By stopping between notes, the student is able to measure distance and focus on weight, speed, and hair contact. Each note should have a good tone quality. Then play without stops maintaining equal volume throughout bow. Adjustments are made when going from lower to upper part of bow in fingers, hand and arm. (To review adjustments, see Section VA). Use the whole bow for each exercise.

D. Combining Rhythms And Bow Distribution At Different Parts Of The Bow

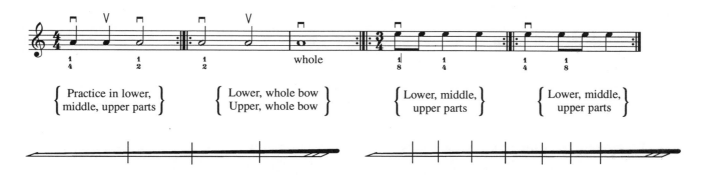

Apply finger, hand and wrist movement to make smooth bow changes. Adjust weight and hair contact when playing in different parts of the bow to equalize tone quality and volume. First practice on open strings, then apply these patterns on A major scale.

E. Early Repertoire Can Be Used To Study Bow Division

Pieces in the early period that are being reviewed and refined can add the study of bow distribution.

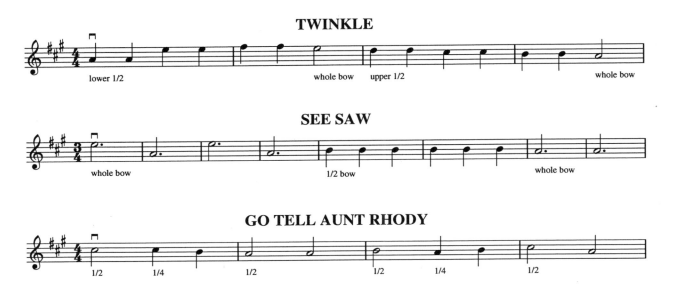

Practice "Go Tell Aunt Rhody" at lower part and upper part of the bow.

VI. LIFT AND RESET MOTION. (REPEATED DOWN-BOW AND UP-BOW STROKES) ["SONG OF THE WIND"] (⊓ ⊓ ∨ ∨)

Exercise:

Place the lower part of the bow on the A string. Draw a down-bow quarter note (⊓♩). Lift bow. Then in a circular motion reset bow carefully on string at the same starting point (in the lower part of the bow). Repeat a down-bow quarter note (⊓♩). The exercise emphasizes freedom of movement of the entire arm and shoulder. This also refines control of the bow hold. Also, practice up-bow strokes (∨ ∨) at lower part of bow with the same kind of circular motion but in an up-bow direction. This is a common bowing and appears at all levels of solo and orchestra repertoire. Repeated down-bow strokes occur for the first time in "Song of the Wind."

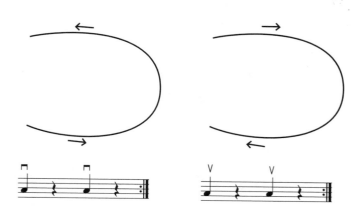

Lift and Reset. [2]

An interesting way to practice this bowing is to select an early piece that is very familiar and can be played by memory so that the primary focus can be placed on this movement which is to be played at the lower part of the bow.

TWINKLE

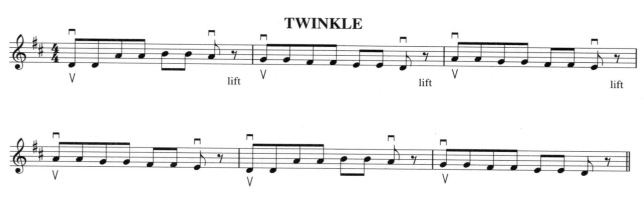

VII. PLAYING IN ALL PARTS OF THE BOW AND REFINING BOW ARM MOVEMENTS ["ETUDE"]

A. When above rhythms are performed correctly and feel comfortable, add different rhythms (e.g. "Twinkle" variations) in each part of the bow. Practice on open strings first, then on an octave scale.

B. Use review and refine pieces to study playing at different parts of the bow.

1. Play entire piece in each part of the bow (upper, middle, lower).

2. Play 2 measures in upper third. Stop. Lift bow to middle part and play 2 measures. Stop. Lift bow to lower third. Stop. Lift bow to middle part. Stop. Lift bow to upper third and play 2 measures, etc. Use lift and reset circular bow arm movement when changing to another part of the bow.

TWINKLE

GO TELL AUNT RHODY

C. In "Bourrée," G.F. Handel (Volume 2) — a more advanced piece, the most common bowings are détaché eighth note patterns. This etude by Sebastian Lee will assist in developing flexible, fast moving left fingers as well as a firm, even-tone-quality détaché bowing. It is a relatively easy etude and should strengthen both hands in a short time. Also, this is an excellent preparation for the more complex eighth note patterns in "Bourrée." When security is achieved at a slow tempo (the tempo used when starting a new piece or a new etude), increase speed gradually. Apply the physical/mental approach controlling movements with slow practice. Clean and agile coordination of fingers and bowing is a desirable goal. Play at middle of bow. When this feels comfortable, play at upper and lower part of bow.

ETUDE

SEBASTIAN LEE

1. Rolland, page 11.
2. Rolland, page 15.

CHAPTER 3
DEVELOPING LEFT HAND AND FINGER DEXTERITY
FROM BEGINNING MOVEMENTS TO ADVANCED TRILLS

I.   BUILDING FLEXIBILITY IN FINGERS IN SEQUENTIAL ORDER

   FROM "PRE-TWINKLE" TO VOLUME 2 PIECES 56

II. DEVELOPING DEXTERITY EXERCISES FROM NEW PIECES. ILLUSTRATION:

   "GAVOTTE FROM 'MIGNON'" BY A. THOMAS 59

III. DEVELOPING EFFECTIVE TRILLS 61

IV. "PERPETUAL MOTION" AND "ETUDE" (VOLUME 1) USED

   AS DEXTERITY EXERCISES 62

V.   ETUDES USED TO PROMOTE FINGER DEXTERITY 62

VI. PLAYING GRACE NOTES 64

CHAPTER 3
DEVELOPING LEFT HAND AND FINGER DEXTERITY FROM BEGINNING MOVEMENTS TO ADVANCED TRILLS

The preceding chapter contains exercises developing flexibility and control in the bow arm when playing in all parts of the bow and on all strings. This chapter concentrates on developing finger dexterity of the left hand. These exercises create agile and energetic finger actions that fall from the base knuckles and are tension-free. They are presented in sequential order gradually increasing in difficulty from simple movements in "pre-Twinkle" songs to the quick actions when playing "Perpetual Motion" and trills. Dexterity exercises should be included in the daily practice schedule as a warm-up for the left hand and fingers. Focus is also on practicing tone quality and a balance of tone throughout the bow when playing 8-12-16 notes to a bow. Different ways to practice dexterity finger movements are included in this chapter.

I. BUILDING FLEXIBILITY IN FINGERS IN SEQUENTIAL ORDER

The goal is to promote equal mobility, independence and strength in each finger. Keep the left hand quiet when fingers are falling and raising with energy. These exercises also keep the hand positioned over the fingerboard.

Play these in strict time. Start slowly and increase tempo gradually over several days. Start these on the A string, but to gain flexibility across the fingerboard, apply on other strings. The left arm and elbow rotates under the violin when changing strings and places the wrist, hand and fingers in the proper position on each string.

The purpose is to develop evenly-played rapid notes on all strings and the playing of runs, trills and turns. Finger agility and strength also help to intensify vibrato movements.

A. Dexterity Exercises While Studying Repertoire

1. Practice daily when studying "pre-Twinkle" songs and into Volume 2.

(a) Left fingers alone. Lift and place each finger on its marker and keep strict time. Movement comes from the base knuckles with fingers nicely curved. The first finger should rest against the fingerboard nut to give support to the hand. Observe playing posture and position of violin with left arm over knee and toes and nose pointing down fingerboard. Also, notice the straight position of hand, wrist and forearm. These exercises help to achieve proper finger placement (with aid of markers) to establish good intonation and spacing of notes in this key. Anchor (hold down) the fingers as indicated to maintain position of hand and fingers over the strings and to set interval spacings. When the interval relationships are secure, eliminate excessive anchors. Exercises without anchor fingers are used to promote independent movements. As agile finger actions develop, increase tempo. Place as much energy in upward as well as downward movements.

Play these same exercises with bow. These exercises are particularly useful when a student is beginning to coordinate left hand, fingers and bowing. First, play with staccato articulation at middle of bow. The short stop after each note gives the finger an opportunity to be placed on the proper marker. Finger first, then bow. As good coordination develops, try playing with smooth détaché bowings without stops. Whether playing staccato or détaché, each note should be the same length with a good tone quality. Practice these when studying the "Pre-Twinkle" songs.

(b) Add the fourth finger. Use left fingers alone. Then bow exercises with staccato and détaché strokes. The fourth finger is introduced when studying "Perpetual Motion." This is an excellent dexterity piece.

(c) When studying pieces at the level of "Minuet 1" (key of G major, Volume 1), use a scale pattern of four notes and start studying slurring by two to a bow with each note receiving the same amount of bow with equal tone quality. The scale is used as a dexterity exercise.

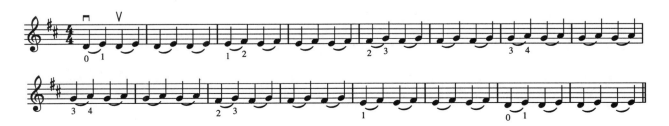

(d) When working on pieces at the playing level of "Gavotte" (key of G major, Volume 1), slur four to a bow. Transfer to D/G strings using same finger/bowing pattern. Use full bow and divide it into four equal parts. Energize finger movements with flexible finger joints.

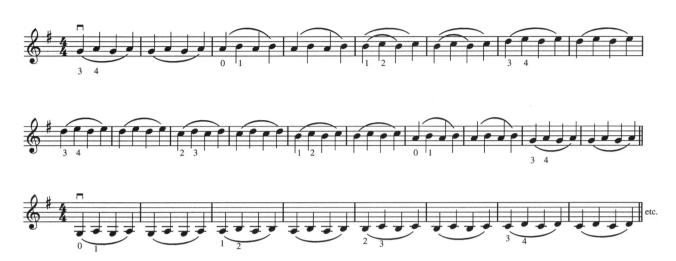

(e) When studying "Minuet 3" (key of G, Volume 1), slur three to a bow and use full bow. Piece is in 3/4 time.

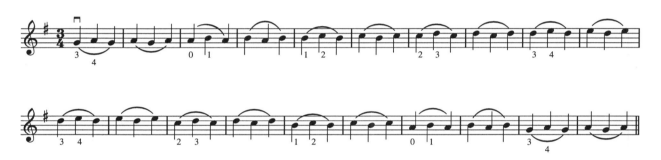

(f) Slur four, then eight to a bow. Concentrate on bow control, agile finger movements and evenness in tone quality and volume throughout the slur. Notice the position of the hand and wrist drawing the bow from frog to tip and from tip to frog. The hand and wrist are higher than the forearm and elbow at the frog (a partial hair contact with bow slanted toward fingerboard). The hand and wrist are about the same level at middle (hairs are flatter) and are at a lower position at tip (full hair contact with bow stick above hairs). To create an even full-bow tone quality and volume, the adjustment of hand and wrist and amount of hair contact must work together. Practice this exercise when working on "Gavotte from Mignon' " by A. Thomas, key of G, Volume 2. This will assist in refining the playing of this piece and the playing of full bow legato passages.

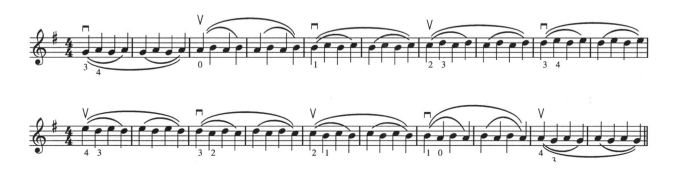

(g) When studying "Waltz" by J. Brahms (key of G, Volume 2) slur three, then six to a bow.

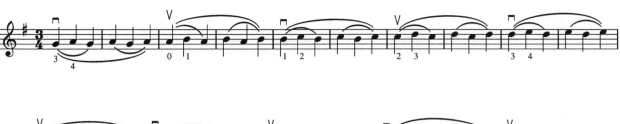

II. DEVELOPING DEXTERITY EXERCISES FROM NEW PIECES

As the repertoire advances in difficulty, the demand for finger dexterity, strength and independence in each finger increases. To prepare for a fast moving passage in a particular piece, select an exercise that facilitates the playing of that piece.

For instance, "Gavotte" by A. Thomas (Volume 2) contains a series of 16th and 32nd note passages which are to be played at a moderately fast tempo.

GAVOTTE FROM "MIGNON" A. THOMAS (VOLUME 2)

This is essentially a trill-like pattern that is used several times from "Gavotte" (Thomas, Volume 2) through Volume 3. It is a common figure that appears in the lively music of the Baroque Period and can be developed in a simple rote exercise played with a minimum amount of tension. This exercise practices two essentials to playing trills: an active finger movement, and a quick solid controlled movement of the bow producing a clear tone quality. Start at slow tempo (adagio) and build to allegretto.

59

The first trill appears in "Gavotte," J. B. Lully (Volume 2).

The final piece, "Minuet," by L. Boccherini (Volume 2) contains a quarter note trill with added grace notes. This occurs on both E and A strings.

Quick finger actions as developed in previous trill exercises coupled with clean bow articulations are present in Dvořák's "Humoresque" (Volume 3). This is a combination of 16th notes and 32nd notes.

HUMORESQUE

A. Dvořák

"Gavotte" by Jean Becker (Volume 3) includes many left hand and finger dexterity, bowing, string crossing, articulation and finger pattern challenges. These techniques that have been explained and studied previously gradually build up to this playing level. In all of these techniques, energetic and quick-acting finger movements are absolutely essential.

GAVOTTE

Jean Becker

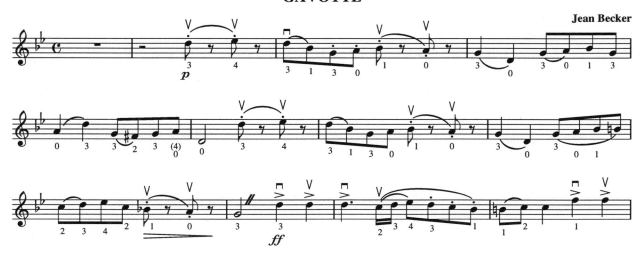

III. DEVELOPING EFFECTIVE TRILLS

One of the most difficult left hand and finger techniques is playing clean, even trills while keeping the hand tension-free and having smooth, controlled bowing. Playing trills requires mobile fingers with action from the base knuckles, with each finger possessing strength and control. This also applies to grace notes, turns and fast 16th and 32nd notes. The dexterity exercises, which start while working on the early pre-Twinkle, "Twinkle" repertoire and continue through Volumes 1, 2, 3 pieces, gradually bring finger agility to the level of playing trills effectively.

Begin this exercise at a slow tempo and gradually increase tempo over a period of time. Keep strict time. A correctly played trill is based upon evenness of notes as well as the number of notes included in the trill.

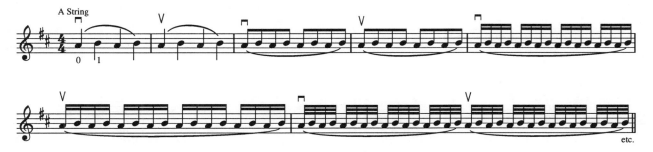

Progress to second, third, fourth fingers, then descend. Start with quarter notes and progress gradually to 32nd notes.

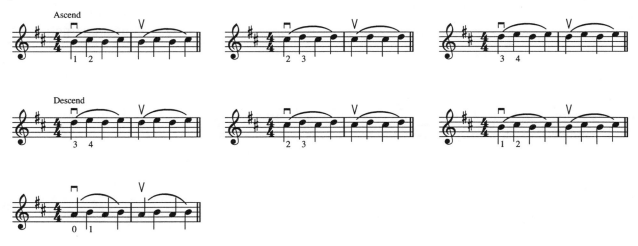

IV. "PERPETUAL MOTION" AND "ETUDE" (VOLUME 1) USED AS DEXTERITY EXERCISES

When "Perpetual Motion" and "Etude" in Volume 1 are being played very well, use them in conjunction with or instead of dexterity exercises. The review and refine daily practice period on familiar pieces can be used by both rote and note-reading students.

Since these pieces are played by memory, special attention can be given to bowing short, even détaché strokes and quick finger movements. Perhaps, the best way to coordinate the bow and left hand is to concentrate on each of these separately. (1) For instance, play each note twice at a moderate tempo concentrating on proper forearm and elbow action, string crossings, even notes and good tone quality. Then repeat focusing on energizing downward and upward movements of left fingers. (2) Proceed to playing single notes. Increase tempo gradually as coordination between bow and left fingers develops.

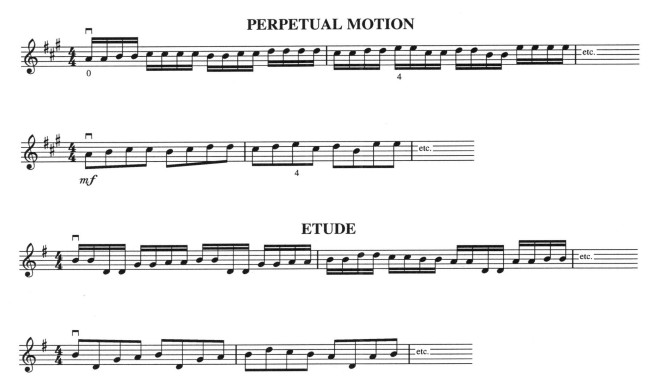

If this procedure is placed in the daily practice schedule, by the time the repertoire is completed in Volume 1, "Perpetual Motion" and "Etude" should reach the level of fast, well-coordinated playing with many bowing and left hand and finger techniques accomplished. Continue these in Volume 2. They can be used as a daily warm-up exercise for both left fingers and bow.

V. ETUDES USED TO PROMOTE FINGER DEXTERITY

As the student progresses technically and with good reading ability, more options are available for technical and musical growth. With the fingers achieving tension-free flexibility through the use of dexterity exercises in various keys, rhythms, tempos and strings in this early period, interesting etudes can be introduced into the daily schedule to advance techniques. These should be placed in sequence and match the level of difficulty of the solo repertoire.

The dexterity etude can be used in different ways: The entire etude can be studied (which takes a longer time to play through and study); or perhaps only half of it. The reason why many teachers suggest only a part of the etude is that it is repetitious and absorbs time in a restricted daily practice schedule.

Also, if the goal is to develop a mastery of what the etude contains (e.g. accuracy of intonation, tone quality, flexibility and speed of bow and left fingers) then this goal may be achieved quicker by practicing a portion rather than the entire work. The choice may depend on the need of the student, the amount of daily practice time and the length of the etude. However, strength and endurance are further developed when studying the entire work.

It is suggested that the fingers drop firmly and rebound quickly from the string. The hand should be quiet and tension-free and not assist the finger in dropping or lifting. Fingers should be curved at all times.

The examples below illustrate how to match levels of dexterity etudes with related repertoire such as in Suzuki Volume 2. This approach of relating etudes to repertoire can be applied to intermediate and advanced levels as well.

When Studying "Musette" by J. S. Bach (Volume 2) key of D major, practice the following section from this etude-like piece and apply bowings that appear in "Musette."

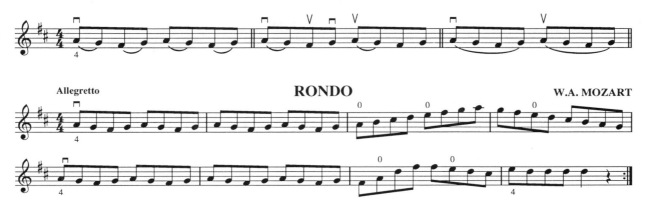

"Long, Long Ago," by T.H. Bayly (Volume 2) contains a large section with the figure ♩♪♪. The following Wohlfahrt "Etude" bowing pattern can be adjusted to serve as a finger dexterity as well as a bowing exercise for this piece.

VI. PLAYING GRACE NOTES

Playing grace notes requires rapid and strong finger action. A grace note is played quickly before the beat with the following note on the beat. The amount of bow used depends on the rhythm of the note that is attached (usually slurred) to the grace note. In "Gavotte," by J. S. Bach (Volume 3), for instance, a quick grace note is followed by a sustained half note all in one bow.

GAVOTTE

At first, leave the grace note out to obtain the proper rhythm, meter and bowing of the melodic line. When the flow of the melody is established, add the grace note.

CHAPTER 4
INTERRELATING REPERTOIRE WITH SCALES, MINI-EXERCISES AND ETUDES

I.   EXPLANATION OF WHAT AND HOW TO INTERRELATE 66

II. EXAMPLES OF INTERRELATING PROBLEM AREAS IN REPERTOIRE WITH

     SCALES AND MINI-EXERCISES TO BUILD TECHNIQUES...67

III. ADDITIONAL EXAMPLES OF INTERRELATING PIECES, SCALES,

     MINI-EXERCISES, ETUDES 72

IV. PREPARING THE ETUDE 77

V.   MASTERING BOWING TECHNIQUES USING "PERPETUAL MOTION"...........................77

VI. GUIDELINES IN DETERMINING AND COORDINATING GRADE LEVELS

     OF INSTRUCTIONAL MATERIAL 78

VII. THE USE OF ETUDES 82

CHAPTER 4
INTERRELATING REPERTOIRE WITH SCALES,
MINI-EXERCISES AND ETUDES

I. EXPLANATION OF WHAT AND HOW TO INTERRELATE

The role of the scale, mini-exercise and etude has had an interesting and highly significant place in violin repertoire. These are generally used as technique builders and are an important part of the daily practice schedule. How and when to use these in relation to the solo repertoire is usually left to the discretion of the teacher. However, a plan is described, herein, that suggests an approach to build musical and technical skills sequentially that is interesting, productive and highly motivational to the student using an interrelated format.

A. Solo Repertoire

Solo pieces should be attractive and inspirational. Knowing this, Suzuki carefully selected excellent solo pieces and generally places them in a sequential order of difficulty based on keys, note values, range, bowings, string crossing, form, length, etc. To assist in working out the problem areas in each piece, he suggests that they be isolated, simplified and carefully studied.

B. The Diatonic Scale

The diatonic scale is very versatile in that it can be used to work on problem areas, many different kinds of techniques and musical expressions such as: finger patterns in the key of the piece to secure intonation and establish tonality, bowings, rhythms, articulations, bow division and dynamics.

C. The Mini-Exercise

"Whenever technical problems are encountered, they must be analyzed to determine the nature of the difficulty: intonation, shifting, rhythm, speed, a particular bowing, the coordination of the hands, and so on, or a combination of several of these. Each difficulty should be isolated and reduced to its simplest terms so that it will be easier to devise and to apply a practice procedure for it."[1]

By using a mini-exercise, a student begins to focus on the difficult areas in a piece, and with guidance from the teacher, learns to locate a problem, and to work it out step-by-step. Thinking critically and developing analytical skills are important parts of learning, accomplished by identifying and extracting a problem, studying it on the open string and working it out with a mini-exercise.

D. The Etude

The etude focuses on a particular technique that needs to be improved and strengthened. This should be at the same level or perhaps slightly easier than the related piece. An easier etude working out a technique will still achieve the same objective with less stress. If it is too difficult, it will consume a great deal of practice time and deter progress. Reading ability must be developed before adding the etude to the practice schedule in order to take part in this cooperative technical building plan.

Note: After problem spots are worked out and the techniques and musical expressions are functioning well in the piece, practice four-measure phrases and eight-measure sentences. This ties the piece together into a logical musical structure and makes the entire piece easier to learn.

To keep interest, learning and progress at a high level, it is advisable to assign pieces just a little more advanced than the previous piece or pieces that may introduce a few new techniques. Too big an increase in technical demands actually slows progress.

II. EXAMPLES OF INTERRELATING PROBLEM AREAS IN REPERTOIRE WITH SCALES AND MINI-EXERCISES TO BUILD TECHNIQUES

A. "Twinkle" (Volume 1) Key Of A Major

1. Scale (work on bowings, rhythms, articulations, finger patterns)

(a) Staccato, détaché (studying both bowings)

Playing the staccato involves a variety of activities in the bow arm. At the beginning stage, Suzuki suggests that the initial staccato be performed legato with stops. A basic bowing movement is to be accomplished first, that is, action by the forearm initiated by a flexible elbow while playing at the middle of the bow. Any tightness or stiff feeling in the upper arm and shoulder should be avoided. To practice the staccato bowing, place the bow on the A string at the middle, apply a little weight into the first and second fingers of the bow hold with thumb pressure against the frog. Then release this weight and return to normal position. Practice this several times to obtain this feeling of weight and release. When functioning properly, place weight into bow, release and follow by a quick draw of the bow, then stop. This completes the staccato stroke.

The staccato and détaché stroke should be the same length (at middle part of bow), using the same forearm and elbow movement, and both producing a good tone quality

The open string exercises listed below are used to study the performance of both staccato and détaché bowings. First, play the staccato notes legato with stops. Then smooth détaché bowings without stops. The weight and arm motion are identical. Then practice regular staccato bowings and articulation and proceed to play smooth détaché bowings on the A major scale. Notice the contrast in executing each one. The détaché stroke plays through the entire value of the note. The staccato: weight ("bite"), release, quick draw, stop. Note value $\flat$ʔ. Study each bowing on the A major scale.

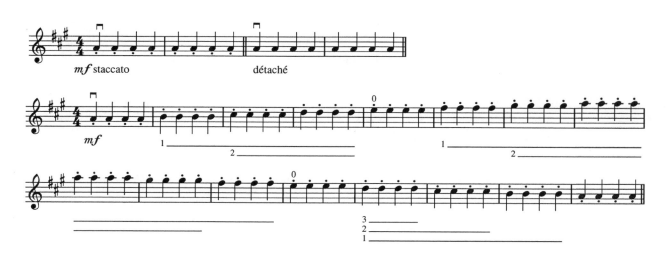

Apply finger anchors building up from the first finger to identify patterns (spacings) for this key. Using the anchors also places the hand and fingers in a desirable position over the fingerboard. This helps to secure good intonation (see section B on use of anchor fingering).

Notice the level of the bow arm when playing on A and E strings. Lower the arm when going from lower to upper string; raise the arm when going from upper to lower string. Keep shoulder joint and upper arm relaxed and flexible.

(b) Rhythms

Study rhythms and articulations on open strings first. Concentrate on proper bowing action of forearm and elbow movements, quick adjustments between détaché and staccato and good tone quality. Then apply on the A major scale to coordinate bow and fingers.

Also:

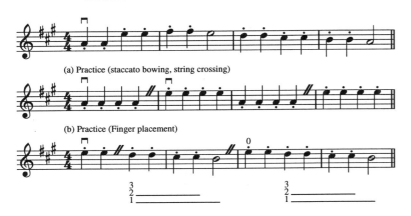

2. Mini-exercise (working on problem areas).

Problem Area:

(a) Practice (staccato bowing, string crossing)

(b) Practice (Finger placement)

(a) First practice string crossing by lowering and raising the arm silently at middle of bow between the E and A strings. At this early stage, the hand and arm move as a unit when crossing strings. Notice the level of arm on each string. Proceed to play the four staccato notes on open A. Stop. Then cross to open E string. Continue exercise stopping the bow before crossing. Strive for a good tone quality with notes evenly spaced. Basic bowing action is forearm and elbow. Refining string crossing with bow arm movements can start when working on "Aunt Rhody." The hand leads the way going from upper to lower string; the forearm and elbow initiate the downward movement of the arm going from lower to upper string. Chapter 2 contains special string crossing exercises. Note value ♩ (played ♪ᵧ).

(b) Finger placement (measurements). Stop when crossing from E to A string. Place first and second fingers down on markers building up to the third finger (note D). Correct placements lead to good intonation. Also, all the fingers are in position for the descending notes.

The above examples indicate how to extract and practice a problem area or study a technique that needs to be strengthened.

Note: When string crossings and finger placements of "Twinkle" and Variations are secure, proceed to use independent fingering which is essential for fluent finger movements. Practice going from open E to third finger on the A string (note D) without including the first and second fingers. At first, stop the bow and set the third finger before changing strings. Gradually, learn to set the third finger without stopping. At this stage of development, the second and first fingers should drop into place as they are needed. The left hand and fingers should be well positioned over the strings.

B. Proper Use of Anchor Fingerings ("Lightly Row")

At the beginning of this study ("pre-Twinkle" into "Twinkle"), finger measurement techniques were used; that is, keeping fingers down from the lowest to the highest note within ascending and descending melodic patterns (2b). The purpose is to establish finger patterns and relationships in the key of the related piece, exercise, or scale. It assists in obtaining good intonation from both a physical and ear-training perspective and keeps fingers nicely curved over the fingerboard and strings. Prolonged use, however, results in a cumbersome action of each finger and creates less finger flexibility. Some teachers will use this approach at the beginning stage perhaps through "Twinkle" or "Lightly Row." By this time, the hand and fingers are nicely positioned and proper spacing of the fingers is fairly well established. Independent actions and placement of the fingers are beginning to develop. Practicing dexterity exercises will add to left hand and finger mobility.

If a student has intonation problems in playing repertoire, keep the fingers over the strings in good playing position, organize finger patterns with related scales and practice more slowly with this measurement approach. After security has been established, eliminate some of these measurement fingers and proceed to use key anchors.

An occasional anchor finger or fingers can remain on the string to help set a position or finger pattern within a melodic passage for more fluent playing, to measure awkward intervals, to aid in crossing strings and when playing double stops and chords. This is an important technique and a great asset when encountering complex passages. The teacher will often indicate bowings and fingerings in a new piece especially at this early stage.

The following are examples of anchor fingering from Suzuki repertoire used to set key fingers in melodic passages for more fluent playing.

"Lightly Row" (Volume 1)

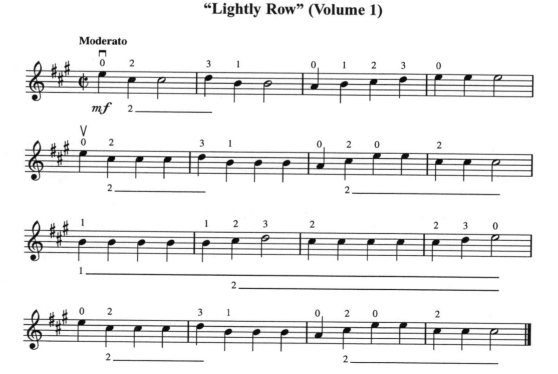

SONG OF THE WIND (Volume 1)

MINUET 2 (Volume 1)

J.S. BACH

WALTZ (Volume 2)

J. BRAHMS

CONCERTO IN A MINOR (Volume 4)
(3rd Movement)

A. VIVALDI

C. "Lightly Row" Volume 1, Key of A Major

1. Scale (practice rhythms and bowings).

    (a) Legato playing

Strive for a good tone quality at middle of bow (forearm and elbow are the primary movements).

    (b) Bow Division

At first, the quarter and half notes are the same length played at middle of bow. To accomplish this, slow down the speed of bow on the half note. Then practice bow division on scale (♪ ♩ ♩) and apply this on the piece.
¼ ½

2. Mini-Exercise (working on problem areas).

    (a) Problem areas:

        - legato playing

        - string crossing

First play four quarter notes on the E string. Stop. Then four quarter notes on the A string. Notice the level of arm on each string.

Now practice rhythm of the piece on the open string, first with equal bow for each note. Repeat using bow division. (♪ ♩ ♩)
¼ ½

Practice

(b) Use of anchor fingers (measures 7-8 and 15-16).

This is an example of an anchor finger which remains on the string while playing open E. This places the hand and fingers over the strings which helps to facilitate the playing of this passage. The second finger is at the center of the melodic pattern.

III. ADDITIONAL EXAMPLES OF INTERRELATING PIECES, SCALES, MINI-EXERCISES, ETUDES

As the student develops reading ability and progresses through the Volume 1 repertoire studying new bowings, rhythms, string crossings, bow division on open strings, scales and mini-exercises, a level of proficiency is achieved when real etudes are introduced. The mini-exercise can still be used to work out problems and the etude will assist in strengthening technical skills. Etude (a French word) means study. Theodore Karp in his *Dictionary of Music* defines etude: "as a piece designed to help the performer develop his/her technical abilities, generally in one particular area. Many etudes are nearly devoid of musical interest and are used only for their mechanical value."[2]

A. "Minuet 2," J.S. Bach (Volume 1). Key of G Major.

1. Scale (G Major). Study bowings and rhythms.

(a) Slurred staccato. For each staccato note, place weight into first, second fingers and thumb of bow hold. Release. A quick draw. Stop.

(b) Bow division with rhythm patterns in "Minuet 2": Practice on G Major scale.

1.  1/2 bow

2. 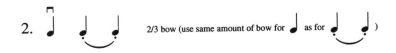 2/3 bow (use same amount of bow for ♩ as for ♪ ♪)

3. ♩ ♫♫ (2/3 bow for ♩) (1/2 bow for ♩ ♪ ♪ ♪)

72

2. Mini-exercise. Problem areas.

(a) Refine string crossings: lead with the hand when crossing to a lower string and lead with the elbow when crossing to a higher string.

(b) String crossing; bow division. When playing the 𝅗𝅥. note adjust weight in bow arm and amount of hair contact to obtain an even tone throughout bowing.

(c) Triplets slurred in one bow. First practice slurred staccato and stop after each note with notes evenly spaced. Then play smoothly as written.

(d) An extended third finger.

Study measurements with anchor fingering.

3. Etude study. Etudes are used to develop and strengthen techniques that appear in a particular piece or in weak areas found in the general playing skill. For instance, when working on "Minuet 2," finger movements, rhythms and bowings in this piece can be studied with etudes which will secure these skills. When they appear again, the student is prepared.

(a) This "Etude" by Hohmann can be used to study the following techniques: eighth note playing with a firm tone at the middle or just above the middle; string crossings. Playing fast passages between two adjacent strings, the crossing action is performed, primarily with the wrist. Anchor fingers are used to facilitate movements within melodic patterns.

ETUDE

HOHMANN

(b) Other bowings similar to the ones used in "Minuet 2" and that also appear in later pieces can be studied on this Hohmann etude.

(c) This is a study in learning to play triplet rhythms evenly. First play with evenly spaced and equal tone quality on each note in $\frac{6}{8}$ time in a moderate tempo (six beats to a measure). Then transfer into a faster triplet pattern ($\frac{2}{4}$ time). This is also a good exercise for dexterity development.

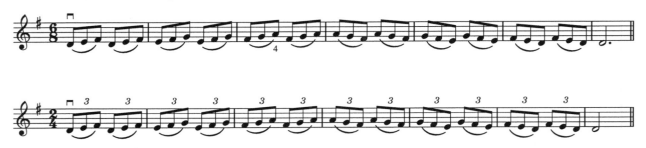

Apply to other strings.

4. Learning form. After the problem spots are worked out, practice a four-measure phrase or an eight-measure sentence. All the bowings, rhythms, articulations and notes that make up the phrase are brought together. It is often easier to remember all of these parts when played within a musical phrase or sentence. Also, phrases and sentences are often repeated. In "Minuet 2," measures 1 and 2 appear six times.

B. "Gavotte" by Gossec (Volume 1), Key of G.

Special techniques to be developed in this piece:

Bowings on scale: staccato, détaché lancé, slurred staccato, slurring.

Mini-Etudes: single and double string crossings, grace notes, fingering problems, finger dexterity, lift and reset.

(**Note:** These must be practiced slowly at first to coordinate mind and hands to study proper motions and tone quality. Gradually increase tempo as security develops.)

1. Scale (working on rhythms and bowings).

(a)

Staccato; middle part of bow. Strive for good tone quality. Every note receives the same emphasis.

(b)

Staccato; alternating thirds. (m. 9, 11)

(c)

Détaché Lancé: a broad staccato with a slight pause after each bow stroke. (m. 2, 4)

(d)

Alternating détaché lancé with regular détaché.

2. Mini-Exercise (problem areas)

(a) Slurred staccato with string crossings. Elbow leads hand going from lower to higher string. Hand leads elbow going from higher to lower string.

(b) Tricky fingering: Keep first finger down throughout passage. When the third is played a second time, lift the second finger and move close to first.

Practice:	Practice:	Practice:
Without bow (pizz.).	Slurred staccato.	Slurring.
Then play with bow.		

1. lift second finger.

2. place second finger to new position.

(c) String crossings (détaché lancé, détaché).

(d) Grace note practice. Play grace note before beat.

(e) Developing finger dexterity with string crossings (even and energetic finger action).

(f) Lift and Reset playing ⊓⊓ (in combination with string crossing, grace note, détaché lancé).

3. Etude. Combining string crossing, slurring, lift and reset (⊓⊓), and two slur/two separate ♩♩♩♩. Keep fingers down where indicated to secure intonation. It also organizes the finger patterns of this work and facilitates finger movements across strings. A flexible left elbow helps rotate the hand and fingers over the fingerboard.

ETUDE

WOHLFAHRT

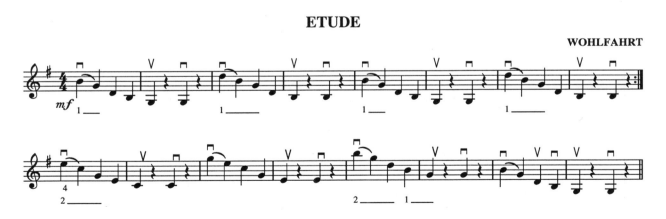

Practice slowly and concentrate on executing proper bowing techniques. All of these have been explained and studied in previous exercises or pieces which should make this etude easier to play. By repeating these techniques and adding new ones from new pieces, the student develops a firm technical foundation and continues to augment playing skills. As the etude becomes secure at a slower tempo, increase gradually. If daily practice time is limited, concentrate on the first eight measures. Benefits can still be achieved.

IV. PREPARING THE ETUDE

As previously stated, an etude emphasizes a special technique that can increase a student's playing ability at a particular time of growth or when encountering a problem in a current piece. Slow, thoughtful practice is encouraged at first to focus on the proper execution of the technique present in the etude. Since the entire etude usually emphasizes the same problem, it is recommended that a small section be studied for a week or to the point where it is almost memorized and feels very comfortable. This speeds up the learning process of the technique rather than studying the entire etude and taking a longer period of time to attain a competent playing proficiency. After security is achieved in the first part, the remainder of the etude can be studied starting with slow practice and gradually increased tempo over a period of time. The etude is now in two different stages. The second part, however, will progress much faster because of the facility accomplished in the first part. If the technique is to help work out a particular problem in a related piece, this approach will advance the playing proficiency at a rapid pace and thereby result in learning the piece more quickly. However, completing the etude is recommended as it promotes in-depth facility, strength and endurance.

V. MASTERING BOWING TECHNIQUES USING "PERPETUAL MOTION"

After studying "Perpetual Motion" in Volume 1, place it into the daily practice schedule to review and refine bowings, rhythms and articulations from previous pieces and add those from the new piece. This is especially suited to students who are still in the rote learning stage. They enjoy this type of exercise because the notes are memorized which gives them greater freedom to concentrate on mastering bowings. They feel progress and control being developed at a faster rate and are better prepared when encountering these bowings in new pieces. Practice new bowings slowly at first and focus on proper execution. When comfortable, gradually increase tempo. It is interesting to study the movement of upper arm, forearm, elbow, wrist and fingers of each bowing when progressing from a slower to a faster tempo. (Refer to Chapter 8 for a detailed explanation of how to perform various bowings.)

As an example, when the new piece is "The Happy Farmer" (Volume 1), the following bowings can be reviewed with "Perpetual Motion" (Volume 1)

77

Dotted notes  "The Happy Farmer"

Note: Using an etude-like piece like "Perpetual Motion" may substitute for a real etude when refining bowings even for more advanced students.

VI. GUIDELINES IN DETERMINING AND COORDINATING GRADE LEVELS OF INSTRUCTIONAL MATERIAL

All through this text emphasis has been placed on interrelating teaching materials (e.g. pieces, exercises, scales, etudes) each developing technical and musical playing skills in different yet cooperative ways. These are all at the same technical and musical level and create a well-balanced and comprehensive program of study for the young violinist. How does one determine the various grade levels? One way is to select a sequentially written string method book which follows the standard guidelines for grading and involves range, key, rhythms, meter, bowings, string crossings, etc. Most method series adhere to this step-by-step format.

When using the Suzuki solo repertoire, which is also presented in a logical sequence of range, keys, rhythms, etc., one can see how this music fits into this system. For instance, the first quarter of Volume 1 can be listed as Grade 1 since the pieces are in duple meter, Key of A major (one octave), simple rhythms, détaché and staccato bowings. Once a piece is graded, it can be coordinated with scales and etudes. Ensemble and orchestra music graded by publishers can also be placed into this graded program (examples are listed in Chapter 11).

Guidelines in Determining Grade Levels

Grade 1 - 2   Elementary

2 1/2 - 4   Intermediate

4 1/2 - 5 1/2   Advanced

6 - 6 1/2   Artist

STRING METHOD BOOKS 1-2-3-4-5 ANALYSIS
[FOR INDIVIDUAL OR CLASS INSTRUCTION]

Book 1: Keys of D, G, C (Grade Levels 1 - 1 1/2)

Range:

1st position
All strings

Meters: $\frac{4}{4}$ $\frac{2}{4}$ $\frac{3}{4}$

Note Values (Rhythms): ♩ ♩ ♩. ♪ 𝅝

Bowings:

(slur)   (tie)   L.H. pizz

Book 2: Keys: D, G, C, F, Bb Eb, A (Grade Level 2)

Range:

 1st position
All strings

Meters: $\frac{4}{4}$ $\frac{2}{4}$ $\frac{3}{4}$ $\frac{6}{8}$

Note Values (Rhythms):

New Bowings:

Double Stops:

Book 3: Keys: D, G, C, G, F, Bb, Eb, A (Grade Levels 2 1/2 - 3)

Range:

 1st and 3rd positions
All strings
Shifting exercises and pieces

Meters: $\frac{4}{4}$ $\frac{2}{4}$ $\frac{3}{4}$ $\frac{6}{8}$

Note values: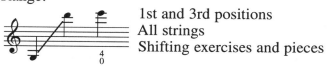

New bowings:

Double stops: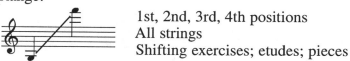

New Position: Introductory Exercises, pieces in third position; all strings and keys.

Book 4: Keys: D, G, C, A, F, Bb, Eb, E; d, a, g minor (Grade Levels 3 1/2 - 4)

Range:

1st, 2nd, 3rd, 4th positions
All strings
Shifting exercises; etudes; pieces

Meters: $\frac{4}{4}$ $\frac{2}{4}$ $\frac{3}{4}$ c $\frac{6}{8}$ ¢

New note values (rhythms):

79

New bowings:

Double stops: same as Book 3

New Positions: Introduction to fourth position; exercises and etudes in 1st, 3rd and 4th positions; all strings, keys.

Book 5: Keys: D, G, C, A, F, B♭, E♭, E; g, d, c♯ minor (Grade Levels 4 1/2 - 5 1/2)

Range:

1st, 2nd, 3rd, 4th and 5th positions
All strings
Shifting exercises; etudes; pieces

Meters: $\frac{4}{4}$ $\frac{2}{4}$ $\frac{3}{4}$ c $\frac{6}{8}$ ¢

New note values:

New bowings:

Double stops: more double stops; add chords

New positions: Introduction to fifth position; exercises, etudes and pieces in 1st, 3rd, 4th, and 5th positions; all strings and keys.

SUZUKI REPERTOIRE - ANALYSIS/GRADED

Volume 1: (Grade Levels 1 = 1 1/2 - 2)

Keys A, D, G (Basic Keys)

Range:

1st position
All strings

Meters: $\frac{4}{4}$ ¢ $\frac{2}{4}$ $\frac{3}{4}$

Note values (rhythms):

Bowings:

Volume 2: (Grade Level 2)

Keys: D, G, C, A, F; g minor, a minor

Range:

 1st position
All strings

Meters: $\frac{4}{4}$ ¢ $\frac{2}{4}$ $\frac{3}{4}$

Note values (rhythms):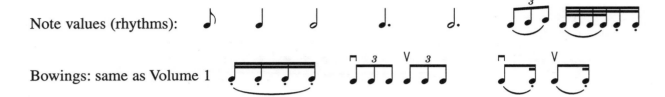

Bowings: same as Volume 1

New techniques: trill; double stops; chords; fourth finger extension

---

Volume 3: (Grade Level 2)

Keys: A, D, G; e minor, g minor

Range:

 1st position
All strings

Meters: $\frac{4}{4}$ ¢ $\frac{2}{4}$ $\frac{3}{4}$

Note values (rhythms): same as above. Also,

Bowings: same as Volume 1

New techniques: same as Volume 2

Volume 4: (Grade Levels 2 1/2 - 3)

Keys: A, D, G, F; a minor, e minor

Range:

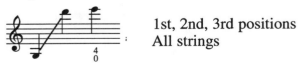 1st, 2nd, 3rd positions
All strings

Meters: $\frac{4}{4}$ ¢ $\frac{2}{4}$ $\frac{3}{4}$ $\frac{6}{8}$

Note values (rhythms): same as Volume 3:

Bowings: same as Volume 2

New techniques: Increase use of double stops; chords; trills; includes 2nd and 3rd position etudes.

Volume 5: (Grade Levels 3 1/2 - 4)

Keys: a minor, g minor; E♭ major

 1st, 2nd, 3rd, 4th and 5th positions

Meters: $\frac{4}{4}$ ¢ $\frac{2}{4}$ $\frac{3}{4}$ $\frac{6}{8}$ $\frac{12}{8}$ $\frac{3}{8}$

Note values (rhythms): same as Volume 3:

Bowings:

VII. THE USE OF ETUDES

The etudes are graded according to levels of difficulty in the same way as the repertoire and string method books. These are an important part of a student's practice schedule to assist in building techniques. Some teachers begin with the first etude and proceed through the entire book. Others will select ones that work out specific technical problems in the solo pieces. In either case when selecting teaching material: the repertoire, method book lessons, scales and etudes should all be at the same grade level.

Etudes for Violin - Graded

Grade 1-2   Elementary

2 1/2 - 4   Intermediate

4 1/2 - 5 1/2 Advanced

6 - 6 1/2   Artist Level

Grade level	Title (author)	Publisher
Grade 1 - 1 1/2 (first Position)	*First Position Etudes for Strings* (Violin, Viola, Cello, Bass, Piano Acc.) (Samuel Applebaum) (Etudes by Dancla, Sitt Arr. Bach, Wohlfahrt, etc.)	Belwin
	Early Etudes for Strings (Violin, Viola, Cello, Bass, Piano Acc.) (S. Applebaum)	Belwin
	First Studies in the First Position, Vol. 1, Op. 25 - The Beginner (Hofmann)	
Grade 2	*20 Etudes in the First Position*, Op. 32, Bk. 1 (H. Sitt)	G. Schirmer
	Etudes for Technic and Musicianship (S. Applebaum)	Belwin
	The Well-Tempered String Player - 55 Etudes (Matesky-Womack)	Alfred
	First Etude Album (Whistler-Hummel)	Rubank
	Foundation Studies, Bk. 1 (Wohlfahrt-Isaac-Lewis)	Carl Fischer
	Foundation Studies, Bk. 1 (Wohlfahrt-Aiquoni)	Carl Fisher
	Orchestra Bowing Etudes (Violin, Viola, Cello, Bass) (S. Applebaum)	Belwin
	22 Studies for Strings (Wohlfahrt-Hohmann)	Belwin
	60 Studies for Violin,. Op. 48. Bk. 1 No. 1-30 (Wohlfahrt)	G. Schirmer
Grade 2 1/2	*Foundation Studies, 4 Studies, Bk. 2* (Wohlfahrt-Aiquoni)	Carl Fischer
	60 Studies for Violin, Op. 45, Bk. II, No. 31-45 (3rd Position) (Wohlfahrt)	G. Schirmer
	Orchestra Bowing Etudes (Violin, Viola, Cello, Bass) (Applebaum)	Belwin
	22 Etudes for Strings (edited by F. Muller)	Belwin
Grade 3	*15 Studies,* Op. 68 (C. Dancla)	G. Schirmer
	36 Studies, Op. 20, No. 1-12 (Kayser)	G. Schirmer
Grade 3 1/2	*20 Progressive Exercises,* Op. 38 (J. Dont)	G. Schirmer
	15 Studies, Op. 87 (R. Hofmann)	International
	36 Studies, Op. 20, No. 13-26 (3rd pos.) (Kayser)	G. Schirmer
Grade 4 - 4 1/2 (5th Position)	*36 Studies,* Op. 20, No. 27-36 (Kayser)	G. Schirmer
	40 Selected Studies, Op. 36, Bk. 1 (Mazas)	G. Schirmer
Grade 5 - 5 1/2 (5th-7th Position)	*16 Melodious Studies,* Op. 128, Bk. II (C. Dancla)	Carl Fischer
	42 Studies (R. Kreutzer)	G. Schirmer/ International
	20 Etudes from 2nd-5th Positions, Op. 32, Bk. 4 (Sitt)	G. Schirmer
Grade 6 - 6 1/2	*36 Etudes* (F. Fiorillo)	International
	24 Etudes and Caprices (P. Rode)	G. Schirmer
	24 Etudes and Caprices, Op. 35 (J. Dont)	G. Schirmer
	24 Matinees (P. Gavinies)	International
	24 Caprices (N. Paganini)	G. Schirmer

EXAMPLES OF SCALE BOOKS

Grade level	Title (author)	Publisher
Grade 1-2	*A Tune a Day Scale Book* (C. Paul Herfurth)	Boston Music Co.
	Scales for Strings, Bk. 1 (S. Applebaum)	Belwin Mills
	Scales in First Position (H. Whistler)	Rubank
	Elementary Scales and Bowings for Strings (Whistler-Hummel)	Rubank
Grade 1-3	*Scale Studies* (H. Schradieck) Carl Fischer	
Grade 3	*Scale Studies* (J. Hrimaly)	G. Schirmer
	Intermediate Scales and Bowings (Whistler-Hummel)	Rubank
Grade 4 - 6 1/2	*Scale Studies* (J. Hrimaly)	G. Schirmer
	Shifting the Position and Preparatory Scale Studies (Otakar Sevcik)	G. Schirmer
	New Scale Studies (C. Halir)	Carl Fischer
	Warm-Up Scales and Arpeggios (L. Kaufman)	T. Presser
	Scale Studies (C. Flesch)	Carl Fischer

Also refer to the graded list of string method books (Chapter 4). All include scale studies.

1. Ivan Galamian, *Principles of Violin Playing and Teaching.* (Prentice-Hall, Englewood Cliffs, New Jersey; 1985), page 99.

2. Theodore Karp, *Dictionary of Music.* (Northwestern University Press, 1983), page 34.

CHAPTER 5
THE SCALE: BUILDING TECHNIQUES AND MUSICAL SKILLS

I.   SCALE STUDIES: DEVELOPING BOWINGS, RHYTHMS, ARTICULATIONS 86

II.   AN OVERVIEW OF BOWINGS, RHYTHMS, ARTICULATIONS FROM
       "PRE-TWINKLE" THROUGH VOLUME 1 86

III.   ORGANIZING A DAILY SCALE PRACTICE 88

IV.   OTHER WAYS TO USE THE SCALE: STUDYING DYNAMICS, TEMPOS, VIBRATO AND
       INTONATION 89

V.   STUDYING FINGER PATTERNS IN DIFFERENT KEYS WITH SCALES 91

VI.   DEVELOPING AURAL PERCEPTION WITH SCALES 92

CHAPTER 5
THE SCALE: BUILDING TECHNICAL AND MUSICAL SKILLS

The renowned violin pedagogue Ivan Galamian states: "The scales have been studied ever since the violin has been played. Their importance lies in the fact that they can serve as a vehicle for the development of a larger number of technical skills in either left or right hand. Scales build intonation and establish the frame of the hand; their applicability for the study of all bowings, of tone quality, of bow division, of dynamics, and of vibrato is almost endless."[1]

The scale, like the etude, has become an important part of the daily practice schedule and a vital resource for developing techniques and musicianship. Galamian indicates the many benefits that can be derived from scale studies: practicing crescendos, decrescendos, tempos, vibrato intensities as well as bowing rhythms, articulations, position study and shifting. All of these solidify skills required for successful performance of repertoire.

I. SCALE STUDIES: DEVELOPING BOWINGS, RHYTHMS, ARTICULATIONS

Daily scale schedule should include these techniques from both current and previous pieces. The keys and range of scales and pieces should match. The teacher should determine a practice plan for the student selecting from the repertoire the bowings, rhythms and articulations to be studied using the scale. If selecting specific bowings (e.g. staccato, détaché, martelé, bow division), for instance, the teacher should illustrate and explain to the student which parts of the bow arm and amount of bow to use for each stroke. The student then "teaches-back" what the teacher said by demonstrating and explaining each bowing to make sure all is correct. The student maintains a mental focus on the proper physical movement and action of each of these techniques and plays tension-free. The teacher can feel confident that home practice will be correctly performed.

II. AN OVERVIEW OF BOWINGS, RHYTHMS AND ARTICULATIONS FROM "PRE-TWINKLE" THROUGH VOLUME 1

When viewing the list in Section B one can see the enormous gain in technical growth when extracting bowing, rhythms and articulations from repertoire and studying them on a scale. Just as pieces appear in sequential order according to level of difficulty, so do the techniques required to play them. Many staccato articulations, for instance, are repeated, but may have different rhythm patterns or are to be played in different parts of the bow. The simple scale serves as a means to work out complex bowing in a new piece. Techniques are learned and the piece progresses at a faster rate. It is impressive to see what and how much can be accomplished by the end of Volume 1 using this coordinated plan between scales and repertoire.

A. "Pre-Twinkle"

For example, in the early "pre-Twinkle" songs, there are two different rhythms and bowings (e.g. ♩ and ♩ rhythms; ♩ staccato and ♩ détaché bowings). The range consists of four notes or half of the A major scale. Practice these first on this four-note pattern to study finger relationships, tonality, the rhythms and bowing articulations. When these basics in both hands are functioning well, playing the songs with good intonation, tone quality and proper rhythms and bowings will result.

Staccato   Détaché   (Also ♩)

B. Volume 1

Listed in this section are examples of a vast range of bowing, rhythm and articulation techniques from Volume 1 pieces that can be studied on scales.

III. ORGANIZING A DAILY SCALE PRACTICE

If a student is starting a new piece like "Allegro," the following bowings, rhythms and articulations in this piece can be studied and secured on the A major scale (the key of this piece).

For the week's assignment, the teacher selects a combination of bowings, rhythms and articulations from "Allegro" and previous pieces to be practiced on the scale. The scale is used to review and refine.

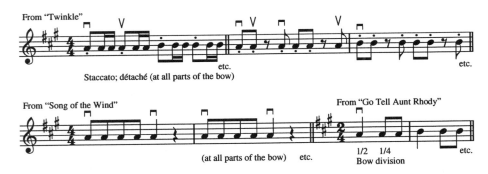

As the repertoire advances, new challenges are added to the practice list and those that are more secure can be studied less frequently. Used in this way, the scale builds left and right hand techniques directly applicable to repertoire. Actually, this simulates a well-designed scale study book.

IV. OTHER WAYS TO USE THE SCALE: STUDYING DYNAMICS, TEMPOS, VIBRATO AND INTONATION

Scales may be used to develop many different kinds of technical and musical skills that are essential to creating effective performance of repertoire.

A. Dynamic Levels

Maintaining the same dynamic level when playing in different parts of the bow requires a weight adjustment in the bow arm and bow hold. At lower part, primary weight of arm is in the second, third, fourth fingers and thumb first finger support. At middle of bow, primary weight comes from the arm into the second, third, fourth fingers and thumb with some additional weight into first finger. At top, primary weight of arm is in first, second and third fingers and thumb with support from fourth finger and more hair contact.

"*f*" (use whole bow at slow tempo); also, "*p*" (use 2/3 bow)

B. Playing Dynamics (e.g. crescendos, decrescendo, piano, mezzo-forte, forte)

Apply principles of weight adjustments listed in Section A. Also, add the following to refine this bowing technique: *Louder* sounds are played near the bridge with more weight placed into the bow, more bow and more hair contact (flatter bow); softer sounds are played near the fingerboard, less weight, less bow and less hair contact (tilt bow stick slightly toward fingerboard). The player should experiment and make adjustments to discover what must be done to achieve the desired dynamic level and still maintain a good tone quality.

1. Study gradual increase and decrease in dynamic levels.

2. Alternating dynamics on a long, sustained note and in the same measure.

3. Dynamic changes in alternating measures.

C. Combining Rhythms

1. Combine different rhythms and articulations at different dynamic levels.

Middle of bow   etc.

Practice these at different dynamic levels: *pp*, *p*, *mf*, *f*, *ff*.

Apply basic principles: (1) short bow stroke for "*p*" less, hair contact and weight in bow, bow closer to fingerboard; (2) longer bow stroke for "*f*" more hair contact and weight in bow closer to bridge.

2. Combine above rhythms and articulations at different parts of the bow (middle, lower and upper parts).

Adjust bow weight when playing "*mf*" at each part of the bow. Apply on the A major scale and rhythms and articulations listed in part C.

mf (middle)   etc. *mf* (lower)   *mf* (upper)

D. Tempos

Selecting from the variety of rhythms previously listed in Section C set a slow tempo for initial practice. Increase tempo as control and security is achieved. When doing so, note the changes in the amount of bow, adjustment in weight, amount of hair and point of contact between bridge and fingerboard.

Apply on all strings: Keys of A, G major:

1. Start with a slow tempo (andante). Repeat scale and increase to a medium speed (allegretto), then play scale at a fast tempo (allegro).

2. At each tempo play "*p*," "*mf*," "*f*" dynamics.

3. Practice different rhythms using different tempos and dynamics.

Also, play rhythm ♩ ♫ ♩ ♫ at middle of bow with a slow tempo (andante) and at a soft dynamic level ("*p*"). Using this same rhythm, play at a medium tempo (allegretto) at a "*mf*" dynamic level. Repeat this rhythm at a fast tempo (allegro) at a "*f*" dynamic level.

E. Vibrato Intensities.

Within each note of the scale, strive to maintain the same intensity (narrow, moderate, or wide). Refer to Chapter 7: Teaching Vibrato With Scale Patterns.

V. STUDYING FINGER PATTERNS IN DIFFERENT KEYS WITH SCALES

When progressing through the repertoire, key changes require adjustments in finger patterns (spacings). Half and whole steps appear in different combinations. In progressing through Volume 1, the first nine pieces are in the key of A major; then two in D major; then six in G major. If a student plays in an orchestra a variety of keys may be presented and adjustments must be made very quickly.

For the young player, it may be difficult to make instant and accurate adjustments when going through a series of different keys. To assist in gaining security, scales in different keys from new and review repertoire should be practiced daily using various rhythms, bowings and articulations for each key. This could have the fingers and bow going through six rhythms and bowings in three different keys. The teacher should tell the student which keys and bowings to practice at each lesson. These may consist of new ones and those that need special attention from previous pieces. Scales practiced in this manner will secure left hand intonation and improve reading facility by keeping patterns of different keys active.

Listed below are scales in various keys from Volumes 1-2-3. Half steps are indicated ($\diamondsuit$).

Volume 1

A Major

D Major

G Major

Volume 2

a minor (melodic)

F Major

C Major

Volume 3

g minor (melodic)

Examples of keys:

Volume 1: D, G, A Major

Volume 2: A, D, G, C, F Major; a minor

Volume 3: G, D, A Major; g, e minor

In a classroom string program, the scale can be an excellent way to coordinate technical develop-ment of repertoire that is studied in the string class and repertoire encountered in the orchestra rehearsal. For instance, a student who starts in third or fourth grade (ages 9-10) and after a year of study wants to participate in an orchestra needs to be in a program that continues to increase basic bowing and left hand playing skills in both lessons and rehearsals. By matching solo and orchestra pieces as to keys, range, rhythms, bowings, level of difficulty, what better way to reinforce and solidify these techniques than by using the scale approach in both lessons and orchestra. Confusion and insecurity often result when les-son and rehearsal pieces are at different levels of difficulty, keys and techniques. Intensive study on spe-cific techniques in small classes and reinforcing them in orchestra accelerates playing skills. The young violinists become highly motivated and encouraged to see excellent progress being made and to be involved in a well-balanced program. (Chapter 4 illustrates how to coordinate solo repertoire, string method books, ensemble and orchestra music.)

VI. DEVELOPING AURAL PERCEPTION WITH SCALES

The scale helps to establish the tonality and the relationship of half and whole steps (intervals) in a new piece. It coordinates the aural and physical aspects of rhythms, bowings and articulations. The ear is not only involved with pitch and tonality, but can also experience the sound of bowing articulations. The ear also directs the physical movements to create the proper dynamic level and quality of tone.

These physical and aural concepts developed on the scale result in a more accurate playing ability.

To keep the aural and physical aspects alive and growing in different keys, review and refine each piece with its related scale. First set the tonality and finger patterns on the scale in the original key of the piece and then play the piece in the same key. Then transpose to other keys. This trains the ear and fingers to make quick adjustments when going from one key to another.

Scale

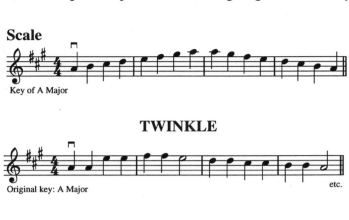

Key of A Major

TWINKLE

Original key: A Major   etc.

Scale

Key of G Major

TWINKLE

Transposed to G Major   etc.

Scale

Key of A Major

LIGHTLY ROW

Original key: A Major   etc.

Scale

Key of G Major

LIGHTLY ROW

Transposed to G Major   etc.   etc.

Final Note: The scale is placed at the center of all phases of technical and musical development by:

1. Reviewing and refining bowings, rhythms, articulations from previous pieces;

2. Studying and refining dynamics, tempos, shifting, vibrato;

3. Studying technical and musical elements in new pieces;

4. Reviewing previously learned keys and finger patterns.

1. Galamian, page 102.

CHAPTER 6
TEACHING CHANGE OF POSITION

I.   INTRODUCTION: THREE BASIC PRINCIPLES OF SHIFTING 96

II.   INTRODUCING PROPER SHIFTING MOVEMENTS OF HAND, WRIST AND ARM 96

III.   COMBINING SCALE PATTERNS WITH "PRE-TWINKLE" SONGS AND VOLUME 1
        PIECES THAT ARE PLAYED IN 3RD POSITION 98

IV.   ASCENDING AND DESCENDING WITH THE SAME FINGER 100

V.   ASCENDING AND DESCENDING WITH DIFFERENT FINGERS 101

VI.   ASCENDING FROM A HIGHER TO A LOWER FINGER AND DESCENDING
        FROM A LOWER TO A HIGHER FINGER (1ST, 3RD AND 5TH POSITIONS) 101

VII.   ASCENDING AND DESCENDING 1ST TO 2ND POSITIONS; ALSO 1ST TO 4TH 102

VIII.   SHIFTING TO DIFFERENT STRINGS (ASCENDING AND DESCENDING) 102

IX.   PLAYING HARMONICS 102

X.   USING REPERTOIRE TO PRACTICE SHIFTING AND PLAYING IN POSITIONS 1-5......104

CHAPTER 6
TEACHING CHANGE OF POSITION

I. INTRODUCTION: THREE BASIC PRINCIPLES OF SHIFTING

1. The ability to hear internally the correct pitch in the new position: the ear should anticipate the higher position. Suzuki calls this a mental/aural image. This should help the hand judge the distance from the lower to the higher position. Descending from a higher to a lower position should have the same assistance from the ear to determine the distance.

2. The mechanical movement and adjustment of fingers, wrist, hand and forearm when shifting needs to be coordinated. The thumb plays an extremely important part in supporting and balancing the violin.

3. When the new position is established, proper finger spacing needs to be determined. As the positions move upward, the spacing becomes closer. Proper spacing insures good intonation.

Each of these three parts will be discussed, with special exercises to help achieve this essential technique. As in any other intricate technique, the questions are: what exercise should be taught, when should each be presented and how should each be taught.

Because this is a complex skill to learn, a step-by-step developmental procedure is included. Some students progress very quickly and accurately and some require much more time and special exercises. The teacher can select exercises most appropriate for each student. String method books usually initiate shifting to the 3rd position in the latter part of Book 2 or in Book 3 with scales, exercises, etudes and short pieces used to study this new position. Shifting introduced by Suzuki appears in the beginning of Volume 4 which includes the 2nd and 3rd positions using scales, exercises and pieces. The first time a change of position occurs (to 3rd position) is in Volume 4, Piece 4, "Concerto in A Minor," first movement, by Vivaldi.

A special Position Etude book by Suzuki introduces shifting starting from 1st position and proceeding through 7th position. It contains scales, exercises and short pieces in each position. Shifting ideas and exercises in the repertoire Volumes plus *Position Etude* can be combined to form an excellent resource in teaching this technique.

II. INTRODUCING PROPER SHIFTING MOVEMENTS OF HAND, WRIST AND ARM: EXERCISING THE SHIFT

This series of exercises introduces the principles of shifting to and from different positions. The most commonly used combination in the beginning stage is shifting to and from 1st and 3rd. Both the traditional string method books and the Suzuki repertoire start shifting between these two positions.

A. Shifting Exercises from First to Third Position Ascending.

The hand, wrist, forearm and thumb shift as a unit with the elbow functioning in a hinge-like motion. Support the violin more firmly with the chin, and the head down and back into the chin rest. Do not tighten or lift the shoulder. The movement should be free of any tension. The thumb should not press tightly against the neck when changing positions, as the ability of the thumb to move freely is extremely important when shifting. The small notes are "guide" fingers shifting. It is suggested that they be played during practice sessions so that the pitch relationships of the different positions can be heard. This trains the aural and physical aspects of measuring the distance between positions. However, in actual performance, the ear anticipates the new position and the glide sound is reduced or eliminated. The sliding finger releases pressure on the string when shifting while the bow moves slower and also releases pressure on the string. If a glissando effect is desired, keep the sliding finger and bow on the string when making a change.

The purpose of this exercise is to practice:

(1) the aural concepts of hearing the pitch of the third finger in 1st position to match the pitch of the first finger in the 3rd position; training the ear to hear (anticipate) the pitch of the new position is basic to a change of position technique;

(2) the spacing between the two positions;

(3) the ascending motion of the hand, wrist and forearm moving as a unit with a flexible elbow;

(4) finger patterns (half and whole steps) in each position.

B. Practicing the Scale Combining 1st and 3rd Positions Ascending and Descending.

The frame of the hand becomes smaller as it progresses to higher positions. The hand and first finger ascend and descend establishing the new position. However, the thumb should precede the hand slightly when descending. The hand, wrist and forearm move together with the aid of a flexible elbow. Notice the adjustment in bow weight between the two positions. As the string becomes shorter in the higher position, more weight is placed into the bow. Playing closer to the bridge will equalize the tone quality between these positions.

C. Exercising the Shift

When the above exercise is performed well on the D string, apply the same shifting movement (1st and 3rd positions) on all strings. The movement should be free of any tension in the shoulder or the arm. A flexible elbow will make this possible.

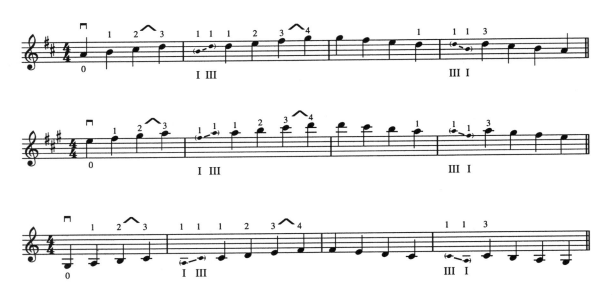

III. COMBINING SCALE PATTERNS WITH "PRE-TWINKLE" SONGS AND VOLUME 1 PIECES THAT ARE PLAYED IN 3rd POSITION

An interesting exercise is to use scale patterns to move from first to third position and proceed to play familiar pieces in the 3rd position. Then shift back to 1st. Apply principles of ascending and descending shifting and adjustments in interval spacing in each position.

Ascending scale pattern

MARY HAD A LITTLE LAMB

Descending scale pattern

Ascending scale

PIERROT'S DOOR

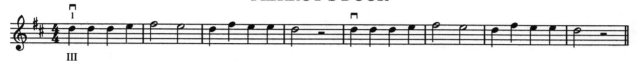

Descending scale

Ascending scale

AUNT RHODY

Descending scale

Ascending scale

TWINKLE

Descending scale

IV. ASCENDING AND DESCENDING WITH THE SAME FINGER

The entire hand moves as a unit. The finger that is down releases pressure on the fingerboard and shifts to the new position. As the hand shifts upward, the primary movement is activated from the elbow with the hand moving parallel to the string. Bow releases weight on the string to eliminate a glissando sound.

Shifting from 3rd to 5th position brings the elbow to the right and the upper part of the thumb to contact the curve of the neck. This moves the hand and fingers to the proper place over the fingerboard, and is the correct position of the elbow (slightly to the right) when playing in upper levels. The frame of the hand becomes smaller as it progresses into the higher positions. The bow moves closer to the bridge.

In descending, the thumb acts as an anchor keeping the hand stable as it moves down. When moving from 5th to 3rd position, the thumb leads the first finger and hand to its proper place. The thumb also leads the hand, wrist and forearm back to 1st position.

Shifting from 1st to 3rd to 5th; 5th to 1st

V. ASCENDING AND DESCENDING WITH DIFFERENT FINGERS

When ascending, the finger that is on the string slides upward until it reaches the new position and helps to measure the distance to the desired note. When descending, the finger that is on the string slides downward until it reaches the lower position. Guide fingers are used to establish the new position.

Basic Principle: When shifting up or down to a different finger, the slide is performed with the finger that is on the string (the finger that was last played).

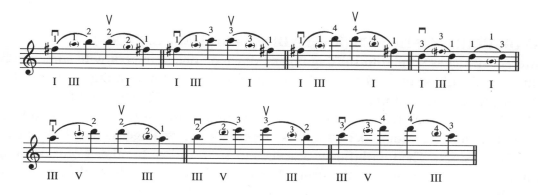

VI. ASCENDING FROM A HIGHER TO A LOWER FINGER AND DESCENDING FROM A LOWER TO A HIGHER FINGER (1st, 3rd AND 5th POSITIONS)

Guide fingers play an important part when developing a change of position technique. As previously stated, they assist in measuring the distance in establishing the new position. The scale can be used to study the proper shifting principles which can be directly applied to repertoire.

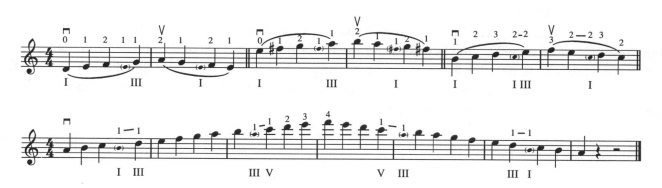

VII. ASCENDING AND DESCENDING 1st To 2nd POSITIONS; ALSO, 1st To 4th

The principles of changing from 1st to 4th position both ascending and descending are the same as shifting 1st to 3rd and 3rd to 1st. The intervals in the 2nd and 4th positions will vary depending on the key. The 2nd and 3rd positions are introduced in Volume 4; the 4th and 5th in Volume 5.

VIII. SHIFTING TO DIFFERENT STRINGS (ASCENDING AND DESCENDING)

Shifting to different strings is similar to shifting up and down on one string but with some modification. (1) The shift up is on the old string and places the second finger on the new string. The bow then crosses over to the new string. The second finger descends to the 1st position. (2) The third finger (which is the last note played in 1st position) shifts upward to set the hand in the 3rd position. The second finger descends back to 1st. (3) The same procedure occurs in this exercise. The first finger is the last played note which shifts to the 5th position. The fourth finger descends to 3rd position. In other words, shifting up or down is performed by the finger that is on the string. Use guide fingers to establish the new positions. Release weight on bow when changing positions to avoid a glissando sound.

IX. PLAYING HARMONICS

In these exercises, shift to the third position and extend the fourth finger either a half or whole step upward as determined by the key. Remove the lower fingers and touch the string lightly with the fourth. This tends to flatten the shape of the fourth finger. It is best to play with the cushion of the finger rather than the very tip for a clearer sound. The harmonic that is produced is an octave higher than the open string. Bowing nearer to the bridge creates a better tone quality.

X. USING REPERTOIRE TO PRACTICE SHIFTING AND PLAYING IN POSITIONS 1-5

"Pre-Twinkle" and early Volume 1 pieces can be used to study proper shifting of fingers, hand and forearm to and from positions, the spacing between positions and the finger patterns in each position.

Position Study with Familiar Repertoire

PIERROT'S DOOR ("PRE-TWINKLE")

TWINKLE

GO TELL AUNT RHODY

SONG OF THE WIND

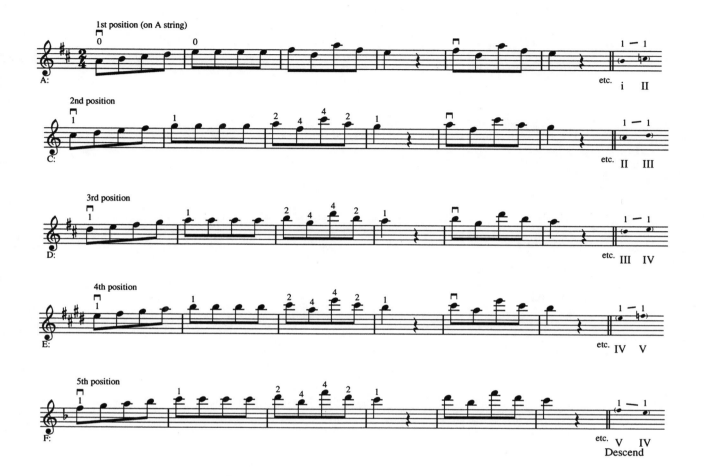

107

CHAPTER 7
TEACHING THE VIBRATO FROM BEGINNING TO ADVANCED LEVELS

I.   INTRODUCTION TO THE VIBRATO...109

II.   BEGINNING EXERCISES: THE HAND POSITION WHEN USING VIBRATO...................109

III.   DEVELOPING THE VIBRATO MOVEMENT OF THE HAND 110

IV.   ADDITIONAL FINGER AND WRIST EXERCISES 113

V.   TAPPING MOVEMENTS TRANSFERRED TO VIBRATO MOVEMENTS 114

VI.   PRACTICING DIFFERENT WIDTHS AND USING FOURTH FINGER VIBRATO 116

VII.   APPLYING VIBRATO ON DIFFERENT STRINGS, WITH DIFFERENT FINGERS
       AND IN VARIOUS POSITIONS 116

VIII. REFINING VIBRATO: PLAYING AT DIFFERENT SPEEDS AND WIDTHS
       ON ALL STRINGS (3rd AND 1st POSITIONS) 117

IX.   DEVELOPMENT OF VIBRATO AS RELATED TO SUZUKI REPERTOIRE 119

CHAPTER 7
TEACHING THE VIBRATO FROM BEGINNING TO ADVANCED LEVELS

I. INTRODUCTION TO THE VIBRATO

Vibrato should be taught slowly and carefully over many months. Even after it reaches an acceptable level for use in playing, it continues to be a technique under constant development. Some students are able to acquire the proper motions almost immediately, but most will need extended preparation and development.

Vibrato is a new experience. It requires new combinations of fingers, hand, wrist and arm movements. The goal is to achieve the most expressive vibrato possible through the use of speed, width and proper application which will enhance the tone and give warmth and beauty to the music. The vibrato plays an emotional and exciting role in expressing music, but its application often results in excess tension in the shoulder, arm or hand which can affect left hand dexterity and bowing facility. Squeezing the thumb against the neck or gripping the violin tightly with the left hand is a common fault. The violin should be supported primarily by the chin and collar bone. The chin exerts a pull on the chinrest toward the neck.

Therefore, it is suggested that easy-to-understand exercises be presented in a sequential manner so that the vibrato can be developed with as little tension as possible. Care should be taken to master each step before proceeding to another. Keep in mind that although a student may understand and demonstrate a movement well, there is still a period of repeated practice needed to develop a motion to the level where it is done automatically with evenness and ease.

When to Begin Vibrato

Vibrato is used to refine the playing of repertoire. However, before this technique is started, the basics should be in place such as: playing posture, bow hold, tone production, bowing techniques, articulations, left hand dexterity, intonation—all functioning properly. When these have been achieved, preliminary exercises can start in Volume 2.

For the beginning vibrato, it is best to develop a hand vibrato with a cooperating movement from the wrist joint. Whatever motion there may be of the forearm will be only a sympathetic movement. Flexibility of the first joint nearest the finger tip is essential. Advanced vibrato will involve an intricate balance of the fingers, hand, wrist, forearm and upper arm. Different combinations of these are used when playing in different positions and with different intensities.

Vibrato in the early stage should be taught in a logical and uniform way just as all other aspects of violin technique. Once the basics are established, more advanced actions can be employed according to the taste of the player and the style of the piece. The teacher can select exercises to fit the needs and level of each student.

II. BEGINNING EXERCISES: THE HAND POSITION WHEN USING VIBRATO
A. Normal Left-Hand Playing Position
The normal left-hand playing position has three contact points: thumb, the base of the first finger against fingerboard and the finger down on the string.

B. Vibrato Playing Position

The vibrato has two contact points: thumb, and the finger down on the string. A vast change occurs when suddenly a lack of support by the first finger places most of the responsibility on the thumb. Additional support can come from a firmer hold of the instrument by the chin. Exercises to practice this new hand position:

1. In 1st position, place left hand in playing position: thumb in place with base of first finger against neck. Place third finger lightly on A string (note D). Now press the third finger into the string. Notice the three contact points. Now release the pressure of the third finger and let it rest lightly on the string. Notice a general decrease of pressure at all three points.

2. Now move the first finger base slightly away from the neck and place the third finger down firmly on the A string (note D). Notice that the thumb must provide all of the counterpressure to the third finger. Keep the thumb in normal position. However, more weight can come from the head into the chin rest to help support the instrument. Repeat this exercise several times a day to become acquainted with this new feeling. The base of the first finger should remain close to the fingerboard. It can touch it lightly but assumes no support to the instrument. As previously stated, the thumb and additional weight on the chinrest take on greater responsibilities.

The first finger should not be too far from the fingerboard.*

III. DEVELOPING THE VIBRATO MOVEMENT OF THE HAND

The basic hand movement should be taught first: the roll of the hand back and to an upright position from a flexible wrist joint. The forearm should not be involved at this early stage. Too much motion from this part of the arm will cause a tight and rigid feeling in the entire arm and shoulder and an undesirable wide vibrato. The forearm will eventually be involved as a sympathetic reaction from a vibrating hand and plays an important part when increasing width and intensities and when in upper positions.

The following exercises will assist in developing the initial vibrato hand movement:

Exercise A

Keeping the forearm resting on a table, tap rhythm patterns with action coming from the wrist joint. Keep fingers curved (as if holding a tennis ball). The impulse motion should come from the wrist joint, not the fingers. This exercise simulates the width of the real vibrato by keeping the hand from going

---

*Playing position and photo as described in The Suzuki Violinist by William Starr. Summy-Birchard, Inc. 1976.

forward. Practice rhythm taps. Tap slowly at first, then gradually increase tempo. Keep strict time. A correctly executed vibrato has a steady, even pulse.

Exercise B

Place the left arm in playing position with elbow resting on a table top. The forearm and hand are in an upright position. Have the right hand hold the left forearm just below the wrist. Now roll the hand in a smooth continuous motion from an upright position, back and then return to the upright position. Do this in even pulses using the following rhythm patterns:

Each upright position is on the beat. The (+) is the backward movement. Start the movement slowly and increase to a moderate tempo. The waist is free of any tension or tightness. The objective is to develop a flexible hand movement which is basic in producing an effective vibrato.

Exercise C: A Tapping Exercise[1]

This promotes agility, aids relaxation and exercises the basic hand, wrist and arm action.

Place violin in playing position with left hand in approximately 5th position with thumb under neck. A tape marker on the fingerboard on the G string on the note F♯ can be used as a guide. With thumb against the bout for support, tap rhythms with second finger with the *primary action coming from wrist*. Start rhythm patterns slowly and evenly. Gradually increase tempo as flexibility develops. Apply same "tapping" (second finger) action and rhythms on other strings in same position. Maintain a tension-free movement in hand, arm and shoulder. Rotate hand and arm position when tapping on different strings.

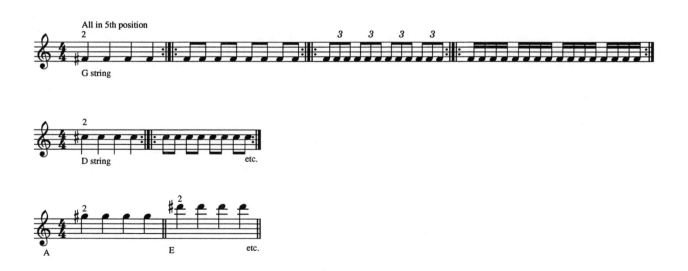

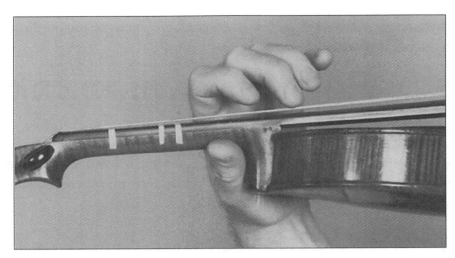

Tapping.

Exercise D. "Polishing" Violin Guitar Position

For further development of hand and wrist movement, place a marker on the fingerboard in 4th position. Then place first finger note E on the A string with heel of hand against the upper right shoulder of the violin. Now lift the first finger so that it lightly touches the string. Keep thumb against neck to support and help balance the hand. Slide finger back about 1/2 inch *with movement of the hand* (from the wrist). Then slide forward to the original position. As previously stated, do not slide hand forward beyond the original position. To make polishing easier, place a small square (one inch) piece of facial tissue between the fingertip and string.

Practice from a slow to a faster tempo: Use wider and slower slides on quarter note and narrow the width as tempo increases. Repeat exercise using second and third fingers. Strive for flexibility of finger joints when rocking back and upright.

Polishing violin.

Note: Vibrato exercises may start in 3rd or 4th position. The 4th is used in this study as it is especially suited to the young student. When in 3rd position with the hand touching the bout, the wrist will bend slightly backward. The 4th position places the hand, wrist and forearm in a straight line which is more appropriate for the backward-upright vibrato motion. This position is more relaxed and will create better movements. Also, the student can easily locate the first finger in 4th position by matching the pitch with the open string next door.

Exercise E

Keep violin in guitar position. Place left hand in first position with second finger on note C# (A string). Move thumb back and forth to release tension and to develop flexibility.

F. Repeat Exercise D (Polishing motion using first, second, third fingers).

With violin in playing position (4th position), polish the first, second, third fingers (E, F♯, G) on the A string: slide slightly back and return to the original position. Do not press into string. Repeat this exercise on other strings (remain in 4th position). Adjust hand, wrist and arm when moving across strings. A very mobile elbow movement gives the hand and arm the freedom to rotate across strings. Now bring the hand down to third position (note D on the A string) and repeat polishing the first, second and third fingers. Slow movements at first, then gradually increase tempo and reduce the width of the vibrato. The primary movement is of the hand while staying in contact with the violin shoulder. Finally, bring hand down to first position on the A string and repeat polishing first, second and third fingers. Practice different widths.

G. Repeat Exercise F (From polishing to firm vibrato).

In 4th position (note F♯ on A string), polish second finger back and to original position. Then gradually (while polishing) place more weight into finger until it is firmly down and begin vibrating. The finger should bend slightly at the top joint as when vibrating. Next, bring hand down to 3rd position (second finger on A string—note E) and repeat the same hand vibrato movement. Finally, move down to 1st position (second finger on A string—note C♯). Apply light pressure on string (while polishing) at first and then gradually add weight and vibrate. Some forearm movement may occur but try to keep it to a minimum. The primary vibrato motion should come from the hand. At a given tempo, each vibrato movement should have the same width and an even back and upward motion.

It starts on the note, with a flexible finger joint, rocks back slightly toward the flatted side of this note. The hand returns to the starting position and the finger assumes its original shape. This completes a vibrato cycle.

IV. ADDITIONAL FINGER AND WRIST EXERCISES

If the student still has problems achieving finger and hand flexibility when vibrating, the following exercises may help.

Exercise A²

Place violin in playing position with left hand in 1st position and second finger firmly down on second string (note C♯). Now place first finger of right hand against second finger. Then vibrate by rocking hand slightly back and to upright position (the original pitch). Work for flexibility in hand, wrist and fingers. Vibrate slowly at first and gradually increase tempo. The right finger trains the vibrating finger to stop in an upright position.

Exercise B

Repeat above vibrating other fingers (first, third, fourth against first). Keep an even motion.

Exercise C

Practice in 4th position with second finger (F♯) on A string. Place finger firmly on string and vibrate. Hand rests against right shoulder of violin. Vibrate slowly at first. When functioning well, increase speed.

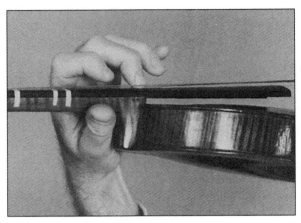

Rest hand against violin in 4th position and practice vibrato at different speeds.

Exercise D (Developing Agile Finger Movements)

Play a major third (first and third fingers) double stop with a long slow bow. Slide the first finger back 1/2 step without shifting or changing the position of the thumb or the third finger, then up 1/2 step to the original position, then up another 1/2 step, then down 1/2 step returning again to the original position. Repeat with the third finger shifting up and down in 1/2 steps.

Repeat exercise sliding second and fourth fingers. Keep all fingers curved. Keep hand tension-free. Start slowly at first. When agile movements develop, increase tempo.

V. TAPPING MOVEMENTS TRANSFERRED TO VIBRATO MOVEMENTS

A. Tap and Bow[3]

Tap an even eighth-note rhythm pattern with the third finger in the 4th position on the D string. Then hold and vibrate. The primary tapping and vibrato motion comes from a flexible wrist with curved fingers. Tapping and vibrato have the same kind of movements. If necessary, the right hand can hold the left forearm to keep the wrist flexible and forearm quiet. When third finger is doing well, tap and vibrate the second. Do not use bow yet; focus on proper wrist, hand and finger action.

B. Repeat Above Exercise (Tap And Bow)

Tap first, then hold and vibrate. Then apply bow with an evenly drawn tone quality throughout note. Keep left hand in 4th position.

C. Apply Same Exercise In 4th Position On The A String.

First, tap even eighth note rhythms, then place finger down firmly, and vibrate. This exercise uses all four fingers. When all four are functioning well, apply bow on string. Tap first, finger down firmly, vibrate, then bow. The vibrato requires an active vibrating hand with a smooth and even draw of the bow.

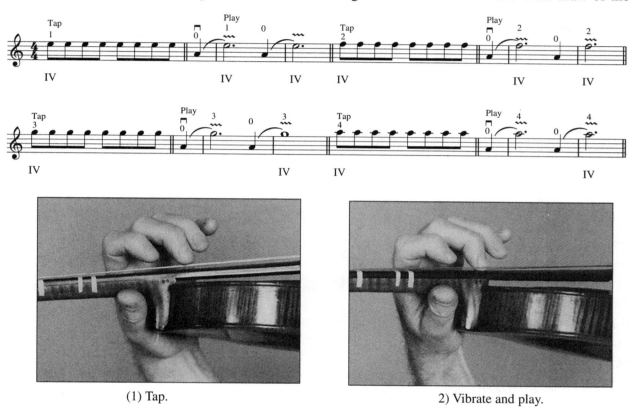

(1) Tap.

2) Vibrate and play.

D. Vibrato Playing in Upper Positions

Vibrato playing in upper positions involves more forearm movement. While in 5th position, make even vibrato movements above the string while bowing on the open string. The thumb (in contact with the violin) serves as a pivot point to support a balanced arm motion. To keep the upper arm from becoming too tight, have the primary movement come from the hand with a cooperating motion from the elbow and forearm.

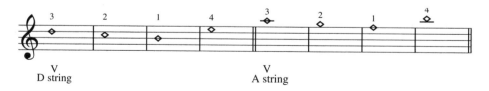

Next, place finger on string, then bow. This exercise also works on the problem of coordinating vibrato playing while bowing and keeping a sustained, smooth tone quality.

VI. PRACTICING DIFFERENT WIDTHS AND USING FOURTH FINGER VIBRATO
A. Vibrate Second and Third Fingers in 3rd Position On The A String.

Perform this action applying three different widths (narrow, moderate, wide). Although the primary action should come from the hand, some arm movement will occur. Count $\frac{4}{4}$ time using four cycles for each beat. Establish a slow tempo, tap foot and count 1-2-3-4 (cycles). Keep strict time. Strive for an even, rocking motion of the vibrating finger/hand.

1. First practice widths without the bow and focus on proper vibrating movement.

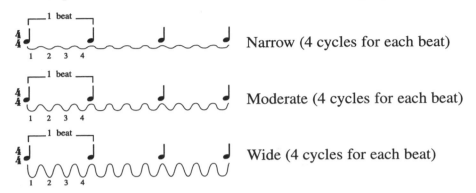

Narrow (4 cycles for each beat)

Moderate (4 cycles for each beat)

Wide (4 cycles for each beat)

2. Apply bow to these three widths with each beat containing four cycles. Keep upper arm and shoulder free of excessive tension.

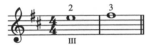

B. Using Fourth Finger Vibrato Requires More Arm Movement.

If student is comfortable with the second and third finger, add a fourth finger exercise. This places the left hand in a rather unbalanced position requiring much more support by the thumb and weight into the chinrest to keep the instrument in place. Much more arm movement is also required as there is less flexibility in the fourth finger joints.

Practice playing   with a narrow, moderate, wide vibrato.

Note: Using the fourth finger will tend to tighten the left arm and shoulder. Try to achieve an effective vibrato with a minimum amount of tension. If student has a problem with the fourth finger vibrato, delay this movement until other fingers are functioning well.

VII. APPLYING VIBRATO ON DIFFERENT STRINGS, WITH DIFFERENT FINGERS AND IN VARIOUS POSITIONS

The previous exercises concentrate on developing basic actions of the left hand, fingers, wrist and forearm. Now that these are functioning well, exercises can be added to expand these vibrato movements in different ways.

A. Play Whole Notes On Different Strings Using Third Finger.

Begin on the A string, then move third finger to D, G, E strings. Adjust hand and arm position when crossing strings. Vibrato movement should be the same on all strings in this position. Sustain vibrato throughout whole note with a good tone quality from bow.

116

B. Repeat With Second And First Fingers.

Introducing the fourth finger is usually delayed until the other fingers are functioning properly and comfortably. As previously suggested, when the fourth finger is used, more forearm movement is involved.

C. Play Whole Notes On A String Using third Finger (Note D).

Then shift to 2nd position playing same note with second finger. Then shift to 3rd position playing same note with first finger. The entire hand moves up as a unit when changing positions. Keep the vibrato slow at first and focus on proper movement, evenness of vibrato and a good sound.

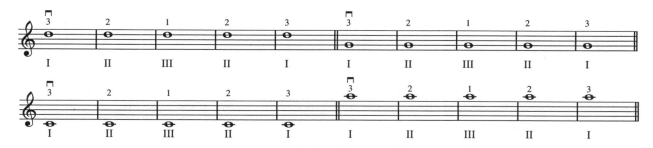

D. Experiment With Different Widths (Narrow, Moderate, Wide) on Other Strings.

Use the same number of cycles (ten) for each note. Practice at a slow tempo.

VIII. REFINING VIBRATO: PLAYING AT DIFFERENT SPEEDS, WIDTHS ON ALL STRINGS (3rd and 1st positions)

A. Use Full Bow When Playing Each Vibrato Exercise.

Apply on all four strings in 3rd position. Maintain an even vibrato and tone quality throughout the bow.

III A String   III D String   III E String   III G String

1. Slow tempo and wide vibrato.

2. Slow tempo and moderate width.

3. Slow tempo and narrow width.

4. Moderate tempo and moderate width (8 widths).

5. Faster tempo and narrow width (10 widths). Bending the wrist slightly toward pegs will help increase the speed of the hand.

6. Faster tempo and moderate width (10 widths).

B. Transpose to 1st Position on All Strings and Repeat Previous Exercise.

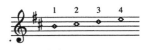

A good vibrato technique can make these adjustments. The tempo and expressive qualities of the piece determine the widths and speeds to be used. "Although it is easier to attain greater speed when the width is small, one must be able to vibrate wide and fast as well as narrow and slow."[4]

C. Explanation Of Speeds (Cycles Per Second) And Widths.
Each cycle is a complete backward and upright movement.

Good Student Vibrato

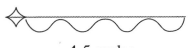

4-5 cycles

Professional Vibrato

6-7 cycles

A good student vibrato is about four to five cycles per second, and at this speed will sound acceptable in pieces. A professional speed, which will vary depending on where it is employed, is about six to seven cycles per second.

A conscious effort to produce a variety of vibrato speeds is necessary. An advanced player can develop changes in vibrato speed with simple exercises previously suggested. How vibrato should be applied in performance can be recommended by the teacher and ultimately, of course, determined by the player. To use, it still is a personal means of expression with a variety of choices in widths and speeds.

Narrow Vibrato: Finger and hand movement with a narrow vibrato is generally used for quiet, less emotional playing.

Moderate Vibrato: Finger and hand movement with some forearm action. Results in a wider and faster vibrato recommended for more intense and expressive music.

Wide Vibrato: Much more hand movement, and possibly forearm movement coming from the elbow, to produce a wider vibrato. Used with music of greater volume, intensity and emotion. Remember to keep the shoulder as tension-free as possible.

Note: The exercises suggest that the vibrato movement rocks the finger back from the basic note (toward the scroll), returns to an upright position and will automatically roll forward which will form a complete cycle. To intentionally force the finger to roll up and be on the basic note will cause intonation problems. The width of a vibrato movement should be the same below and above the basic notes (e.g. narrow, moderate or wide).

IX. DEVELOPMENT OF VIBRATO AS RELATED TO SUZUKI REPERTOIRE

A responsible teacher will determine when the aforementioned "basics" are functioning well so that the study of vibrato may be introduced. Age and proficiency are also factors.

Volume 1: Most students should still be focusing on tone production, intonation and tension-free playing. So much must be accomplished during the first two volumes.

Volume 2: Preliminary vibrato motions as described in this chapter may be introduced. Establish security of the violin at the shoulder and free motion of the left hand by sliding fingers up the length of the string and back. Develop basic vibrato movements of the hand and wrist and apply to the violin.

Volume 3: Work with vibrato tones in the higher position (third or fourth) and move back to first position. Practice scales and slurring two pitches. Apply to the longer notes in Volume 1 & 2 pieces. Continue exercises and reasonable application as repertoire is expanded.

Volume 4: Apply vibrato to slow tonal sections of pieces, legato sections of the Seitz concertos and familiar pieces in the first three volumes. By Volume 5, the vibrato should be fully developed, ready to apply to slow movements of Vivaldi concertos and able to bring out expressive qualities.

1. Rolland, page 43

2. Rolland, page 43

3. Rolland, page 43

4. Galamian, page 42

CHAPTER 8
BOWING ARTICULATIONS

I.   DÉTACHÉ 121

II.   STACCATO AND SLURRED STACCATO 122

III.   MARTELÉ 123

IV.   SUSTAINED MARTELÉ 124

V.   SPICCATO 124

VI.   TREMOLO 126

VII.   SAUTILLÉ 127

VIII.   SFORZANDO 130

IX.   HOOKED BOWING 130

X.   ACCENT 131

XI.   PORTÉ 131

CHAPTER 8
BOWING ARTICULATIONS

The violin is capable of producing many tone colors, dynamic levels and articulations. The beauty and character of a piece is created by the proper use of different parts of the bow arm. The player must understand what is indicated by the composer and the style of the piece, and interpret this with appropriate articulations and dynamics. This chapter will explain the bowing techniques required to play various articulations. Each will be explained in the following ways: A general definition, how each is played, with exercises, scales and repertoire used to study each one.

I. DÉTACHÉ ♩ ♩ ♩ ♩ . A smooth bow stroke played on the string with no visible or audible accent. A separate bow is used for each stroke with the tones smoothly connected. There is no written marking to indicate the détaché stroke. It may be played in any part of the bow.

A. How to Play

The bow remains on the string with natural weight coming from hand, elbow and arm into the second and third fingers. The first finger should not push into the bow as this can result in an unpleasant tone and tightness in the arm but gives support and control to the bowing movement. In the upper half of the bow, movement is primarily of the forearm and elbow. It should open and close the arm as though it were on a hinge. There is a slight upper arm action. The flexible fourth helps to control the bow stroke.

Below the middle of the bow, the forearm and elbow still initiates the movement, and the upper arm moves in and out. However, the upper arm should feel airborne and not tense. Keep shoulder flexible and, as previously stated, the weight on the bow comes from the arm into the middle fingers. The forearm, elbow, hand and wrist move going upbow and downbow as a unit. Make smooth bow changes ⊓ ⊓ ∨ ∨ using wrist, finger and hand action. See Chapter 2 for exercises developing this bow change flexibility.

Common problems: The elbow joint is stiff and the upper arm is too active causing crooked bowing and a harsh, tight sound. This also results in a stiff shoulder joint causing tension in the entire arm.

B. Exercises To Practice Avoiding Excessive Pressure By The First Finger

1. Place middle of the bow on the A string with a regular bow hold. Then lift the first finger off the bow so that the natural weight of the arm comes into the middle fingers (second and third) and thumb which actually form the center of the bow hold. Start with the A string and apply to all strings. Observe adjustments in position of bow arm when changing strings as well as the adjustment of arm weight on each string. This exercise also develops strength and control of the second, third fingers and thumb with support by the fourth finger.

2. Play the above exercise at the middle of the bow with first finger *on the bow*. The natural weight of the arm into the middle fingers and thumb continues as the primary means of creating good tone qual-

ity. However, the first finger does help to control the bow and places additional weight when playing in the upper, lighter part.

C. Scales

Play scales with a regular bow hold, at middle, upper half and lower half of the bow. Keep all fingers on the bow. At middle, the natural weight of the arm goes into the middle fingers and thumb. Add weight into first finger at tip. At lower part, add more arm weight into thumb, third and fourth fingers. Notice weight adjustment when playing on different strings. Keep volume at same level when playing from lower to upper notes.

When increasing dynamic levels, place more arm weight on bow, more hair contact on the string and move bow closer to the bridge. To play softer, use less weight on bow, less hair contact and move away from the bridge. Also, play at a lighter part of the bow (middle to upper half).

D. Repertoire

Refine détaché bowing by reviewing "Twinkle," "Lightly Row" and "Perpetual Motion." Play at various parts of the bow and apply bowing techniques and dynamics described in Section C.

E. Smooth Bow Changes

Refer to Chapter 2: Exercise in developing hand and finger movements. Practice finger, hand and wrist flexibility when changing strokes. Use the G major scale in Section C at middle of bow at a slow tempo.

II. STACCATO AND SLURRED STACCATO

The staccato is a short, stopped note played with the bow in constant contact with the string. The duration of the note is shorter than its written value (e.g. written ♩ played ♪ 𝄾). Each stroke is prepared by applying slight weight (bite) on the bow before beginning the note and then quickly releasing it followed by a quick draw. However, some weight should remain on the bow during the draw to maintain a firm tone.

A. How To Play

Do not place weight on the bow stick with the first finger alone as it will usually result in a scratchy quality and cause tension in the forearm. Apply a little more weight into first and second fingers with thumb pressure against the frog for each staccato articulation, whether playing separate notes or several in a slur.

The slurred staccato requires a small hand action to help move the bow along with first, second fingers and thumb after a quick weight and release for each note. Best place to play the upbow slurred staccato is in the upper part of the bow. Downbow slurred staccato is played in lower to middle part of bow. Actually, there is very little release of weight between notes as the bow keeps "biting" and moving. Many players execute the downbow slurred staccato by turning the wrist slightly downward (stick tilted toward player).

B. Exercise: Weight and Release

Practice placing weight into the bow with first and second fingers with thumb pressure at the point of contact with the frog. Do not play. Just apply weight and release. The fingers and thumb relax after each note. When this action is functioning well, play a series of staccato notes on the open strings with bow. Strive for a good sound and not one that is too stiff or harsh. The basic action comes from the elbow and forearm. Do not tighten upper arm or shoulder. Use middle part of bow.

C. Place Scales
Separate and slurred staccato.

D. Repertoire
Play "Twinkle," "Lightly Row" with separate staccatos.

Play "Twinkle" with slurred staccatos (2/4/8 to bow).

III. MARTELÉ (♩ ♩ ♩ ♩ written; ♪⁷ ♪⁷ ♪⁷ ♪⁷ played).

This is similar to the staccato; however, the initial "bite" (weight) is greater with a very firm draw. It is often referred to as a "hammered" stroke. It also (as the staccato) ends with a clean stop. The dynamic level is louder (*f*, *ff*) than the staccato and played closer to the bridge with more hair contact. The notes are marked with a heavy wedge dot (♩). The bow remains on the string at all times.

A. How To Play
After the initial bite is made, which is performed by weight of the arm coming into the first, second fingers and upward pressure of the thumb, it is quickly released with a simultaneous draw of the bow. The third and fourth fingers are on the bow and add support and control to the stroke. More bow with a more percussive start is used on the martelé than the staccato. The basic action comes from the forearm and elbow although the upper arm moves slightly in and out with each up and down bow stroke. Eliminate any tight feeling in the shoulder. This articulation is usually played in the upper half of the bow. The "grand" martelé is played with 1/2 - 2/3 bow. Like the staccato, the martelé is stopped after each stroke and receives half the value of the written note. The amount of bow used depends on the length of note and tempo.

B. Exercise: Weight (Bite) and Release
Use the same exercise as in staccato (IIB). However, apply more weight into the first and second fingers and thumb, which comes from the arm. Press into the bow. Do not play. Then release. When this action is functioning well, play a series of martelé strokes on the open strings. The timing of weight

(bite)-release is an important part of this articulation. The basic movement comes from the forearm and elbow, but because more bow is used than the staccato, the upper arm is more involved. Do not tighten the shoulder joint. Best playing location is from middle to upper part of bow.

Weight and release (Bow on string)   Play with bow

C. Play Scale

Practice martelé stroke loud (f) and firm.
(grand martelé - ff). Use 1/2 - 2/3 bow.

D. Repertoire

Apply martelé on "Twinkle".

An interesting exercise is to play "Twinkle" with a staccato bowing and follow it with a martelé stroke as a contrast.

IV. SUSTAINED MARTELÉ ( ): An expressive détaché stroke that has a martelé start. It is marked ( ). Whatever articulation is used on the martelé applies to this stroke except that after the attack is completed, the short note of the fast martelé is replaced by a long sustained tone. The bow slows down into a détaché-type draw at any desired speed (depending on note value). Bite—release—sustain. Practice on scale and repertoire.

French Folk Song

The bite is made through the weight of the arm coming into the first and second second fingers and thumb—same as in the martelé stroke with support and control by third and fourth fingers.

V. SPICCATO ( ) A controlled bow stroke which is dropped on the string and rebounds off the string after every note. It usually responds better just below the middle or in the lower part of the bow when attempting a broader effect at a slower tempo. Short, fast and more percussive sounds might respond better toward the middle or slightly above it. Because each note requires an individual impulse and control, there is a tempo limit to this type of articulation.

A. How To Play

Spiccato means bounce in Italian. Each bounce is controlled with the primary action coming from the forearm and upper arm with active involvement of fingers, hand and upper arm. The arm should be light and balanced as the fingers and hand control the pulse. In a slower tempo, the forearm and upper arm participate more with less action from hand and fingers.

Spiccato consists of both horizontal and vertical movements. If the arc is flatter ⌣, the result is a rounder, softer and fuller tone. It is more of a horizontal arc. If a percussive crisper sound is needed, a more vertical movement is used ⌣· If a faster tempo is indicated, more finger and wrist action with less arm involvement and a narrow vertical arc close to the string is used. The wrist and arm are held slightly higher than in détaché playing. The dynamics and quality of tone will be affected by the height of the bow's drop. The more percussive sound, the higher the drop. Under all circumstances, keep shoulder free of an excessive tight feeling. Spiccato bowing may or may not be marked with editorial dots.

B. Exercise

1. Hold bow about 4 inches above A string. Drop bow just below the middle onto the string and allow it to rebound with a turn of the wrist like the turning of a door knob. This creates a vertical movement. Each bounce should be identical in sound and movement.

2. Now, bounce bow with an arc-like motion by the hand and wrist and a cooperative movement by the forearm and upper arm. Keep shoulder joint mobile.

Practice slower and faster tempos with guidelines of proper movements listed above in "How To Play." Also, practice exercise on all strings and adjust arm position when changing strings.

C. Scale

Play a two-octave G major scale which includes all strings. Practice it at a slow tempo using a flatter arc in lower part of bow producing a rounder, softer and fuller tone. Then increase tempo for a crisper sound. To accomplish this, play toward middle of bow with a higher vertical drop with an increase in wrist and finger action and some arm movement. Use more hair contact for a quicker rebound. For a very percussive sound, raise bow higher with a vertical drop closer to the frog. This is predominantly an arm movement.

D. Repertoire

Apply controlled spiccato on early pieces such as "Lightly Row" and "Song of the Wind." Play softly and slowly at first. These are excellent pieces to study spiccato bowing when crossing strings and doing lift and reset (⊓ ⊓) as in "Song of the Wind." As security and control develops, increase tempo and move toward middle of bow. The student should experiment for the best sound location and bow response for each tempo change and dynamic level.

Lightly Row

etc.

Song of the Wind

etc.

VI. TREMOLO ( ). This is a fast, unmeasured détaché-like bowing played with very short strokes in the upper part of the bow. If a louder dynamic level is required, move nearer to the middle where the bow is heavier and the wrist action more flexible. Because this bowing is played at the upper part of the bow, students often stiffen the arm and tighten the shoulder to try to obtain the proper effect. This results in a weak tone quality with limited dynamic possibilities as well as creating an inflexible arm movement, especially when crossing strings. This bowing appears more in orchestral than in solo repertoire. However, it is an important technique and, incidentally, can serve as an excellent preparation for sautillé playing (refer to sautillé bowing Section VII). These rapid moving strokes should be played throughout the duration of the note.

A. How To Play

The action is similar to bouncing a ball. Primarily a flexible finger, hand and wrist movement. Some movement in forearm, elbow and upper arm will occur but keep arm finger and shoulder free of excessive tension. The wrist should be slightly lower than the hand when playing at the upper part of the bow.

B. Exercises

To help loosen the wrist (which is the basic motion for this bowing) play a moderately fast, light tremolo with very short strokes at the upper end of the bow with only the first, second fingers and thumb holding the bow and the other fingers removed from contact. When the feeling of looseness and control is well established in the finger, hand and wrist, add the other fingers.

Practice this exercise on open strings with only first, second fingers and thumb. Do not stop motions when crossing strings. Adjust hand, wrist and arm levels when changing strings. Repeat exercise with all fingers on bow.

Playing tremolo.

C. Scale

1. Play a scale using different dynamic levels. Keep tremolo going when changing notes. Soft playing at top of bow (*p*, *mp*), louder playing a little lower and near middle of bow with more weight into the bow (*f*). More hair contact and playing closer to the bridge will help increase volume. Playing toward fingerboard and less hair contact and weight will decrease volume.

2. An interesting exercise is to play this scale starting soft (*p*) with a crescendo going up the scale and a decrescendo going down the scale. Start at top of bow with light weight on bow (*p*). Move toward middle with more weight on bow coming through first and middle fingers to forte (*f*). When descending, move toward the tip and decrescendo to a piano (*p*). Also, adjust position of bow and amount of hair contact.

3. Play above scale starting (*f*) and decrescendo to (*p*) at top of scale $\diagdown\diagup$. Adjust weight from middle (*f*) to top of bow (*p*).

VII. SAUTILLÉ (♩ = 138-152+ marked (♪ ♪ ♪ ♪)): A kind of jumping bow on each note which is done by the resiliency of the rebounding bow rather than individual lifting as in spiccato bowing. It is best played around the middle of bow; a little below the middle for a slower and louder effect; a little above the middle when playing faster and softer. The exact location depends upon the flexibility and control of the bow. The execution of the sautillé is related to the détaché bowing. However, there is a certain speed or tempo that needs to be achieved before the bow will begin to bounce. Sixteenth notes at mm ♩ = 138-152+

will respond with a bounce and should be played at or near the middle. A slower bounce can be produced at mm ♩ = 90 at a point closer to the frog. The flexibility of the bow is essential in securing an effective sautillé. It is difficult to bounce a heavy or small size bow (e.g. 1/4 or 1/2 size). A young student who is playing a 1/2 size violin and is having problems with the sautillé should use a fast détaché which is an excellent preparation for this bouncing bow. In fact, the short, fast détaché can be used if a sautillé is difficult to produce. The effect can be made to sound like a fast sautillé. Common problems: wrist is too stiff; an incorrect and inflexible place on the bow.

A. How To Play

If the movement of the bow is horizontal (parallel to floor), it will not bounce. This is a détaché movement. However, by applying a circular motion, which is a rotary action from the hand and wrist, the bow will begin to bounce. Some rotary action will also appear in the forearm. A larger circular motion will create a higher bounce. If a faster, smaller one is needed, a narrow circular motion is used.

Slight Bounce   High bounce

When playing with down-bow sautillé, the hand, wrist and slight forearm rotary action are clockwise. Up-bow strokes are counterclockwise rotary actions.

Down-Bow   Up-Bow

B. Exercises

To develop proper actions for sautillé playing.

1. Play a small-size fast détaché (♩ = 138) near the middle of the bow and then turn the stick so that it is above the hair and all of the hair contacts the string. Do not hold bow too tightly. Now play the same fast détaché but add a combination of horizontal and vertical (circular) motions with fingers and hand movement with action generated by the wrist. The bow hold is primarily balanced between the first, second fingers and thumb with other fingers supporting the bow lightly. A good exercise is to hold the bow with the first, second fingers and thumb, and lift the third and fourth fingers. Start with the bow on the string playing a fast détaché. Then create a circular motion with the wrist. As the bow begins to bounce, add the third and fourth fingers. The fourth finger can or cannot be used depending on the response and control of the bow.

2. Using the tremolo may sometimes lead to an effective bouncing bow. Place bow near tip and play a tremolo. Gradually move bow toward middle while continuing the tremolo bowing until it reaches a point where the bow begins to bounce. The forearm initiates the movement while the circular motion of the hand and wrist creates the bounce.

3. A simple exercise to practice this rotary movement:

(a) Apply bow hold to pencil in the normal playing position of bow. Make back and forth détaché movements with flexible fingers, hand and wrist in a horizontal movement.

(b) Move wrist, hand and bow-pencil up and down from wrist in a vertical movement. All fingers must be curved with a light bow hold.

(c) Now move wrist in a circular motion for down-bow strokes clockwise ↶. For up-bow strokes, move wrist in a counter clockwise motion ↷. Notice some forearm movement in both actions.

(d) Replace pencil with bow and place on A string a little below middle. Practice (sections a-d). Start at a slow tempo (mm ♩ = 60) with 16th détaché notes and gradually increase with a circular motion and a slow bounce (mm ♩ = 100). Then into a faster and smaller bounce (mm ♩ = 138+).

C. Scale

The scale and arpeggio can be used to study this difficult bowing. Besides developing the proper bow stroke, coordination between each bounce and left hand fingers is a real challenge. So is trying to maintain a clean, even bounce when crossing strings.

Start with détaché in an on-the-string horizontal bowing. As tempo increases, add a vertical, circular motion. Incidentally, the wrist is slightly slanted downward, more so than for the détaché or spiccato stroke First, practice four bounces to each note; then two bounces; then one bounce. Delay the one bounce per note until the two-bounce note functions well and has good bow and finger coordination. mm ♩ = 60 (détaché) ♩ = 90 (détaché) ♩ = 90 (détaché) ♩ = 138+ (spiccato bounce)

Adjust elbow and arm levels when crossing strings. Elbow is lowered when going from lower to upper strings. The hand and elbow are raised going from upper to lower strings.

D. Repertoire

The foundation of sautillé playing starts early in a student's repertoire with the development of a good détaché. The sixteenth note variation in "Twinkle" (♪♪♪♪ ♪♪♪♪) is well suited for this purpose. In the daily practice schedule, older pieces are constantly reviewed and refined. Reviewing and refining not only strengthen a particular technique but can also serve as a means to accomplish playing skills for more advanced techniques. As previously stated, the sautillé is basically a fast détaché with an added circular motion by the fingers and wrist. The sixteenth note variation in "Twinkle" as well as scale practice can lead to an excellent spiccato bowing, assist in coordinating fingers and bow, and serve as a finger dexterity exercise. First use a fast détaché. Then apply sautillé with a circular motion.

"TWINKLE VARIATION"

Transpose "Twinkle" variation to D/A; G/D strings. Adjust arm to different strings. If a sautillé cannot be fully developed, continue with a fast détaché. The coordination of bow and fingers at a fast tempo should be the basic goal. The sautillé will come eventually as mastery of bow arm and left hand develops. Both "Perpetual Motion" and "Etude" are excellent pieces to practice fast détaché and spiccato bowings.

VIII. SFORZANDO *sfz* *sfz* :

There is an accent at the beginning of the note with a sustained draw for the entire value of the note. It is similar to the heavy accent of the martelé to start the stroke. The bow, however, is drawn in legato style for the duration of the note. The amount of accent before the beginning of the stroke and the volume of the drawn tone depend on the dynamic level. The weight for the accent comes from the first and second finger bite on the bow and thumb pressure against the frog.

Common problems: The pressure is not immediately released resulting in a loud scratching and crunched sound; or not enough bite on the accent (*sfz*) which loses the effect of this bowing technique.

IX. HOOKED BOWING :

This bowing is a combination of a détaché and a staccato played in the same bow. However, it can consist of different combinations of note values. The first note is usually a longer détaché which is played for the duration of the note. Then a brief stop is made to set up the short staccato (first, second fingers weight on the bow with thumb pressure against frog). Used in "Happy Farmer," and "Witches Dance."

Practice different combinations on open string (all strings); then practice on scale.

Practice slowly at first and focus on proper execution. As security develops, increase tempo.

X. ACCENT ♩ :

This is similar to the articulation of the sforzando but with a lighter accent at the beginning of the note. Immediately after the accent, the weight is released and the bow is drawn in legato style for the duration of the note. The amount of accent depends on the dynamic level and style of piece. The weight comes from the first and second fingers on the bow and thumb pressure against the frog. The accent is also used with other types of articulations. The player should identify each one and articulate correctly.

1. A regular accent ♩ is an accent followed by a détaché stroke.

2. This is an accent ♩ with a broad détaché (more bow and a faster stroke).

3. This combines an accent and staccato articulation ♩. Start with a quick accent and then a short, brisk staccato draw. Stop after every note. Reset first, second finger and thumb in the bow hold for the next accent. Usually it is played at a higher dynamic level (*f*). Adjust weight on each string (a little more weight on lower strings) and position of bow arm.

XI. PORTÉ (POR-TAY) (♩ ♩ ♩ ♩).

Although the value of the notes may be the same, the porté indicates that the note should stand out with more expression or emphasis. It is marked with a dash. To obtain this effect, apply additional bow speed and weight at the beginning of the note and sustain it for the full value. The added weight comes from the arm into the middle fingers of the bow hold.

MINUET 2 (Volume 1)

This is an interesting passage to study since it contains several different types of bowings and articulations: porté, staccato/porté, slurred staccato, détaché, bow division, string crossing. Study these separately with mini-exercises and a G major scale to focus on proper execution of each one until each is performing well. Then play the passage as written, slowly at first, being careful to perform it accurately.

Scale

Porté

Porté, slurred staccato, bow division

MINI EXERCISE

Porté, slurred staccato, bow division, string crossing

CHAPTER 9
TEACHING AND PRACTICING

I.   ESTABLISHING AN APPROACH TO TEACHING..134

II.   ESTABLISHING A CORRELATION:

      COORDINATING THE MENTAL/PHYSICAL FOR EFFECTIVE EXECUTION..............134

III.   SUGGESTIONS FOR THE DAILY PRACTICE SCHEDULE.....................................135

IV.   PREPARING FOR ENSEMBLE AND ORCHESTRAL PLAYING 139

V.   SUGGESTED PROGRAM OF STUDY FOR YOUNG PLAYERS 139

VI.   PEDAGOGICAL GAMES..140

CHAPTER 9
TEACHING AND PRACTICING

I. ESTABLISHING AN APPROACH TO TEACHING

One of the most important aspects of effective teaching is a well-organized approach to technical and musical development. An achievable progression of ideas that are easily grasped is a great motivating factor for inspiring students to practice and enjoy their musical experience.

Suggestions in Designing a Pedagogy:

A. Determining what order of technical and musical development: that is, to know *what* techniques lead to the next; the knowledge and execution of one helps to understand and execute the one that follows.

B. Knowing *how* to teach each technical skill in the most effective and efficient way by explaining and demonstrating in a clear, precise manner is absolutely essential.

C. Carefully selecting appropriate repertoire that is interesting, yet productive: knowing *what* to teach and *when* to teach it. This includes a collection of pieces, exercises, scale systems and etudes that are arranged sequentially and interrelated, with each contributing in a special manner. Suzuki repertoire was selected for this study because it is arranged to develop techniques and musicianship in an orderly manner. Musical and technical skills learned in earlier pieces serve as a foundation for pieces that follow. Many teachers use the Suzuki repertoire as is, or insert other pieces. Other teachers create their own sequential listing of pieces. Whatever the case may be, it is imperative that repertoire be selected carefully. Effective teaching is the result of intelligent planning.

II. ESTABLISHING A CORRELATION

When teaching a skill there must be a clear mental image of the proper physical movements necessary to successfully accomplish a particular technique.

"For all types of technical practice, the principle of mental preparation is of paramount importance. It means that the mind always has to anticipate the physical action that is to be taken and then to send the command for its execution."[1]

Galamian refers to this mental-physical relationship as correlation. "The better the correlation, the greater the facility, accuracy, and reliability of the technique."

An effective teacher instructs the student how to apply muscles and joints for the proper execution of a particular technique. For instance, the correlation of specific muscles and joints in the bow arm is explained when teaching the martelé stroke, or the shift from 1st to 5th position, or string crossings. (Previous chapters explain this mechanical, physical coordination to various techniques and how each is acquired.)

To help establish this mental picture of a physical movement, the teacher may illustrate on the instrument and explain in simple terms what physical movements are involved in a particular bowing. Then the student is asked to repeat this so as to become actively involved in a critical thinking, problem solving process. Passing along to students an approach to solving problems is the mark of an excellent teacher, and results in a productive learner.

III. SUGGESTIONS FOR THE DAILY PRACTICE SCHEDULE

Each student should be presented a daily schedule by the teacher indicating what and how to practice. The student is taught how to work out and study problems in a piece: extracting, isolating and analyzing and then finding ways to overcome problems by simplifying them with open string study, mini-exercises and application to scales. At the intermediate level, regular etudes can be used that contain technical problems which can assist in strengthening the technique.

Coordinating special exercises, scales, mini-exercises and etudes, with each one helping the other, teaches the student to see how to use related sources to achieve a desired goal. In time, the student learns to coordinate all of these resources resulting in a productive practice schedule. Slow practice where the mind directs the physical movements in a new piece is absolutely essential. For instance, a new technique repeated several times with mini-exercises brings it into a subconscious and automatic response. As tempo is gradually increased this well-trained mental and physical involvement keeps everything under control and played with confidence.

Previous pieces that are being performed very well through review and refine can be used to study new bowings, contrasting dynamics within and between phrases, bow division, using different parts of the bow, etc.

Example of a Daily Practice Schedule:
A. Review Of Previous Pieces.

Technical problems have been worked out with special exercises, mini-exercises and scales and are functioning very well. The focus is now on tone quality, phrasing, increasing tempo, etc. Working toward a musical goal, a polished performance and playing with ease are motivating and fun to do. Perhaps the greatest benefit is that it solidifies learned techniques which serve as a basis for upcoming new techniques. Refinement and mastery is achieved. A piano accompaniment or the teacher playing a second part provides musical enjoyment and ensemble experience.

B. Working On Current Pieces.

This category may contain one or two pieces depending on the length of each, the available practice time and the learning rate and ability of the student. This repertoire has been moved up from category C (learning a new piece). Most of the problems have been isolated and the techniques are developing very well with mini-exercises, scales and etude study. Now is the time to bring all parts together. Perhaps the best way to do this is through musical groupings or through studying the form of the piece. Noticing sections that are repeated makes the piece easier to learn. For example, in "Twinkle" there are basically only two different sections: The form is ABA in 12 measures. After problem areas are worked out with mini-exercises, each section should be repeated three or four times. Each section (A-B) contains its own technical and musical characteristics such as string crossings, bowings, rhythms, etc. When all sections are performed well the entire piece is put together. Techniques have been achieved and the musical form learned. In a short time, "Twinkle" can be moved to Category A (review and refine).

C. Learning A New Piece.

The student looks forward to starting a new piece and this enthusiasm may be discouraged if the piece contains a great many new problems and requires a long, strenuous period of practice before satisfactory results can be accomplished. Students progress at different rates, and new pieces should be selected accordingly. This step-by-step approach of introducing some new challenges that are achievable within a reasonable period of time moves the piece along more quickly. The firm foundation built through the mastery of the review and refine repertoire will make the new piece easier to learn.

This is where new problems are extracted and practiced with simple exercises, open string study, scales, mini-exercises and etudes. After the new techniques are functioning well, sections can then be practiced. In a short time, the piece can move into Category B where sections are practiced and then the entire piece is played.

D. Note Reading.

The ability to read music requires an understanding of the notation which in turn dictates what is to be played on the instrument. This is a complicated process especially if the young student is trying to learn the physical mechanics of playing at the same time. Perhaps some simple and interesting pre-reading activities can be introduced at the beginning stage while learning basic bowing and left hand techniques by rote.

The pre-reading program can be started with a series of rhythmic movements and singing experiences. A Dalcroze eurhythmic and aural skills program builds an excellent base for the intrinsic feeling of rhythm, meter and melody. It also makes learning to play an instrument easier when there is a direct application of these musical concepts to the physical placement of fingers on the fingerboard and the rhythmic movement of the bow arm.

Listed below are examples of applying eurhythmic and aural skill activities to technical and musical development on the instrument, as well as how these activities assist in reading and interpreting notation. These examples can be modified and adapted to the individual teacher's approach to pedagogy.

1. Pre-reading experiences in the preparatory period (rote teaching).

(a) Start by marching or clapping in time (meter) while singing the words and melody on pitch to the "pre-Twinkle" songs with piano accompaniment. This coordinates pitch, rhythm and meter. The response to these concepts progresses rapidly from piece to piece. This activity can continue from these early songs into Volume 1 (e.g. "Twinkle," "Lightly Row"). All the songs are learned internally before they are applied to the instrument.

(b) The next step is to apply eurhythmic and aural skill activities to the left hand. With the instrument in playing position, place fingers on markers and pluck a four-note scale pattern (e.g. A string, notes 0-1-2-3). This outlines the finger/note pattern of the piece.

Tap foot in time (meter) and pluck the notes (melody and rhythm) to "pre-Twinkle" songs and "Twinkle." Pizzicato is played by placing the right thumb on the end of the fingerboard and using the first finger to pluck the string. The internal development of the melody and rhythm of these songs with eurhythmics is extremely helpful when fingering these songs on the instrument. The student can see how intrinsic learning can benefit the physical aspects of playing. A combined focus is on proper playing position, posture, left hand position, finger placement (pitch), rhythm and meter. All is being coordinated.

(c) The next step is to concentrate on developing proper bowing movements and to coordinate bowing the rhythms of these songs, singing the melody (pitch) and tapping the foot (meter). This is done through silent bowing over the left shoulder. All songs are played in the middle part of the bow. Special attention should be on maintaining a proper bow hold, a flat straight position of the hand, wrist and forearm and a very flexible elbow movement. The shoulder joint and upper arm should be free of any tension or tightness.

(d) The final step is to combine left hand and right hand bowing using the same pieces as in steps (b) and (c).

2. Note Reading Begins.

(a) Visual Identification. Flash cards can be used to identify fingering of notes written on the staff, locating them on the instrument and then plucking the notes to hear the pitch. Notes should be placed on the treble staff in the key of A Major which is the key of the "pre-Twinkle" songs and pieces that appear in the first part of Volume 1. At first, these should be all quarter notes and a range of an A major octave scale. Step (b) will introduce other rhythms.

Pluck these two scale patterns first when viewing them on a flash card.

Then pluck the note or notes which appear on each card.

(b) Note reading should include an easy-to-learn rhythm system (rhythm and meter). There are many different ways to teach these important concepts. An interesting approach that includes both rhythm and meter is the "tap and ta" system. The tap represents the meter and can be performed by clapping the hands or tapping the foot. The ta is spoken and represents the rhythm (duration of notes). Exercises can be written on staff paper, flash cards or chalk board and practiced without the instrument.

The following are rhythm and meter exercises: #1, 2, 3, 4, 5 are written out indicating how this is used; #6, 7, 8 are to be read by the student. These rhythms appear in early songs. Then proceed to tap and ta "Allegro" (#9) which is notated. Other songs can be added from Volume 1 and tap and ta these as illustrated in the "Allegro" piece.

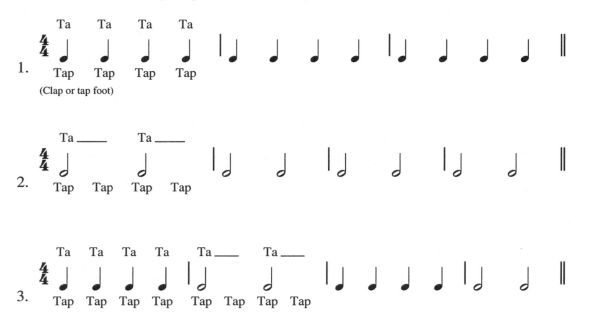

137

4.

Rhythms from Repertoire:

5.

6.

7.

8.

ALLEGRO

9.

(c) Read "pre-Twinkle" songs (notes) playing pizzicato on violin and tap foot to keep time. Next pizzicato "Twinkle" and Variations. This combines note reading (melody and rhythm) and tapping (meter). When reading with pizzicato playing is progressing to a comfortable level, the teacher can play a second part or a piano accompaniment. Chapter 1 contains these "pre-Twinkle" songs with parts.

(d) Read "pre-Twinkle" songs (notes) with silent bowing (bowing over left shoulder) while tapping the foot (combines rhythm and meter). Use a piano accompaniment and/or have the student sing the melody. Continue with "Twinkle" and Variations. The basic bowing movement comes from forearm and elbow working together. Maintain a tension-free action.

(e) Finally, read and play "pre-Twinkle" songs on violin and progress to Volume 1 "Lightly Row" combining left hand and bow. Continue tapping foot to keep a steady beat.

Tapping the foot may not be the approach many teachers or students select. Clapping the meter can be used as an alternative. By clapping and saying "Ta" before playing these early songs, the student will still have an effective way to outline the rhythm and meter. Resource A illustrates the different ways to apply the Dalcroze method of aural and rhythm skills to Suzuki repertoire.

(f) Proceed to a string method book to continue developing reading and playing abilities. These books introduce and explain notes, rhythms, bowings, keys, articulations, shifting, tempos, dynamics, etc. in sequential order using exercises, scales, short pieces and etudes. Reading ability enables students to learn new repertoire on their own and prepares them for an ensemble and orchestra experience. Reading can start at age six when regular reading in school usually begins. It should start when the proper playing posture, good left hand and bowing techniques are attained. If properly taught, these should be fairly well established when completing, for instance, "Perpetual Motion" especially if Volume 1 is preceded by a well structured preparatory period. If a student starts at age three and progress is good, by age six, playing should be in Volume 2 (e.g. "Gavotte," J.B. Lully) or more. Reading should advance at a faster rate. Progress will vary with age, amount of practice, dedication and innate abilities.

(g) An excellent note reading series is *Quick Steps to Note Reading* by J. Frederick Müller, Harold W. Rusch and Lorraine Fink (San Diego Kjos Publishing Company,: 1979). It consists of four books starting with an easy-to-learn approach in Book 1 and a gradual increase in difficulty. What makes these interesting are the scale and rhythm exercises applied to short pieces. Included are duets and trios with second violin and piano parts which present an enjoyable ensemble experience. Several pieces are similar to the ones in the Suzuki volumes applying what was learned by rote to reading the notes.

IV. PREPARING FOR ENSEMBLE AND ORCHESTRAL PLAYING.

A most exciting experience for a young string player is to play in an ensemble and make music with friends. The real fun occurs when a sound technique and note reading ability has been secured. A well-constructed reading program should produce an excellent orchestra player.

V. SUGGESTED PROGRAM OF STUDY FOR YOUNG PLAYERS

It is extremely important that the teacher design a program of study that is interesting and motivating and promotes the growth of each student at an optimum rate. A program should also contain an enjoyable social environment which shares this wonderful experience of making music with other students. By working together, students are encouraged by others and learn from each other.

Example of Activities:

Private Lessons: Learning new left hand bowing techniques; refining techniques; learning how to work out problems in new repertoire with mini-exercises, exercises, etudes, scales; knowing how and what to practice to overcome problem areas and improve skills; increase reading ability.

Technique Class: An emphasis on technical development of bowings, rhythms, shifting, tone study, articulations, etc. using special exercises, scales, etudes. Each class should be at the same level of playing competence. The teacher explains, demonstrates and observes the class work out techniques together. Students learn from each other making this a cooperative learning experience. A student who is slow to understand can learn quickly from those who conceive at a faster rate. This accelerates the teaching and learning process. Of great advantage is that the teacher does not need to devote that much time in individual lessons working on particular techniques that can be covered in this type of class.

Repertoire Class: The study of repertoire that has been and is being studied in private lessons. This class is usually grouped according to levels of ability and knowledge of repertoire. It reviews and refines older pieces to focus on style, interpretation and mastering techniques. Also, it provides an opportunity to do things together. A few more advanced students can participate and serve as helpers and can play a second part creating an ensemble experience for the younger players. One of the incentives and goals of this class is to prepare for recitals.

Ensembles: Duets and quartets of the Suzuki repertoire are available. This introduction to ensemble playing helps to develop the technique of playing with others and establishes an exciting musical and social experience. With note reading taught in the private lesson, a string orchestra can be formed with students involved at all levels of ability. Very easy parts can be arranged for the elementary level players.

VI. PEDAGOGICAL GAMES

Used to accomplish the following:

Mastery: Creative repetition leads to mastery. Like language learning, technical and musical aspects need to be repeated over and over until they are mastered. The physical (muscle development), musical, and mental aspects are learned a step at a time — adding new parts gradually, like building blocks.

Motivation: Games help to develop creative repetition. Instead of playing the same piece many times over in the same way, day after day, vary the approach by using games. Looking at the same thing in different ways keeps the material fresh, interesting and challenging. Because students enjoy the games, repeating the melody is not boring. In fact, students like to repeat, for they see improvement and security.

Social Development: Most of the games are shared with other children, parent or teacher. Sharing an activity is always fun. Participating in the same activity helps students work out problems together.

1. Each student plays 1 measure at a time (pizz. or bow).

2. Teacher points to different students to play one measure.

3. Add on: Teacher selects a starter and points to student (one at a time) to join in. Starter and others continue. All end together.

4. Students turn back to teacher. All students play tune. Teacher taps a student on the back who in turn stops playing. If teacher taps the non-playing student again, that student joins in.

5. "Concerto grosso" style: One student is soloist and plays through entire piece while others play alternating measures.

6. One student is a soloist (bowing) while other pizz. rhythm of piece on open string as accompaniment.

7. Partner songs: Divide class in half — one side plays "Mary Had A Little Lamb," the other side plays "Hot Cross Buns" at the same time. This can be applied to any two songs that are in same key with same number of measures and should be matched as closely as possible harmonically.

8. Bach "Double Concerto" style: Divide class in half (facing each other). Each side plays different song (e.g. "Mary Had A Little Lamb"/"Hot Cross Buns"). Teacher pushes student from "Mary Had A Little Lamb" to "Hot Cross Buns" side with that student shifting to "Hot Cross Buns." Make sure that there is always one student at "home."

9. Clap Hands: Divide class in half. Teacher starts one group. At any time, the teacher claps, the second group continues while the first group drops out (e.g. "Mary Had A Little Lamb"—clap on third beat to prepare incoming group for the next measure).

10. Playing and fingering one another's instruments (while partner holds instrument).

11. Conversation with student while student is playing.

Scale Variations

1. Students select own rhythms and bowings.

2. Play scales in contrary motion, canon style, dynamics, tempo changes, "watch the conductor."

Ear Training Development

Teacher turns back to student and plays note which is within range of notes learned by student to this point. The student matches notes. Rhythm and bowing can also be used. Student can be the teacher (reverse roles).

1 Galamian, p. 95

CHAPTER 10
PLAYING DOUBLE STOPS AND CHORDS

I.   INTRODUCTION 142

II.   EXERCISES TO FACILITATE DOUBLE STOP PLAYING 142

III.   DOUBLE STOP EXCERPTS FROM SUZUKI REPERTOIRE 145

IV.   PLAYING CHORDS 146

V.   PLAYING ARPEGGIOS WITH DOUBLE STOP FINGERINGS 148

CHAPTER 10
PLAYING DOUBLE STOPS AND CHORDS

I. INTRODUCTION
There are two basic principles for effective double stop and chord playing.

A. The Precise Placement and Relationship of Left Hand Fingers
The use of proper finger spacing has been suggested from the very beginning. From the "pre-Twinkle" songs and into the regular repertoire, keeping hand and fingers over the fingerboard and using occasional anchor fingers to establish interval relationships have formed a foundation for double-stop and chord playing. The lower note(s) sets the position and the upper notes are measured from these lower anchor fingers. It is a new experience for the fingers and the ear to play and hear two or more notes at the same time. Simple exercises in this chapter introduce this new aural and physical experience by anticipating, hearing and establishing note relationships.

The left fingers should not press down too hard nor be too tight. This could extend into the wrist and thumb which would keep the hand from playing through double stop passages with ease.

B. Proper Bow Weight and Execution.
The bow should be placed with a little more weight on the lower string which is thicker. This helps to create a balanced sound between the lower and upper strings. Playing closer to the fingerboard is recommended because the strings are at a more even level. For more volume, add weight to the bow from the arm through the middle fingers while playing closer to the bridge. Either excessive weight, a tight bow arm, or not enough bow can cause a harsh tone quality. Do not tighten the shoulder. Bow control is extremely important. The bow must be drawn evenly and smoothly across the strings.

Note: Many teachers use double stop exercises to increase left hand and bowing skills. They place the left hand and fingers in a good playing position, assist in practicing finger relationships between notes, promote flexibility in fingers across strings and help in developing bow control.

II. EXERCISES TO FACILITATE DOUBLE STOP PLAYING

A. Obtaining A Good Tone Quality On Both Strings
For smooth playing, keep left hand fingers on the string as long as possible in double stop passages and draw the bow evenly across strings. As previously suggested, to attain a balanced sound between the two strings, a little more weight on the lower string may be necessary.

Start the exercises listed below at a *mf* dynamic level. When an even sound is achieved at this level, practice different dynamics (e.g. *p, f*). To increase the volume, place the bow closer to the bridge with more hair contact on strings and an increase of weight into the bow. For softer tones, tilt the bow slightly toward scroll for less hair contact on the string, and play closer to the fingerboard. This exercise offers experience in bow placement on strings, weight in bow, amount of bow for each stroke, amount of hair used and production of an equal volume and tone quality between the notes.

B. Mixing Single Notes With Double Stops

When crossing to upper strings, lead with the elbow; let the forearm, upper arm and hand follow. When crossing to lower strings, lead with the hand with the upper arm and forearm following. This exercise introduces string crossings with weight control and adjustments over four strings going from single notes to double stops. Try to maintain the same volume and smooth tone quality throughout the exercise.

C. Combining Slurred Single Notes With Double Stops

Keep bow close to both strings when playing the single notes so it is in a good position to play the double stop. Just roll the bow over from string to string.

D. Playing Consecutive Single Note and Double Stop Patterns

Practice string crossing, bow control from single notes to double stops and adjusting the bow weight when playing on different strings. Also, practice the lift and reset motion (⊓ ⊓). Apply on other string combinations (G/D, A/E).

E. Playing Different Combinations of Slurred Notes (four in one bow)

Balance sound on both strings with smooth legato playing. Use whole bow.

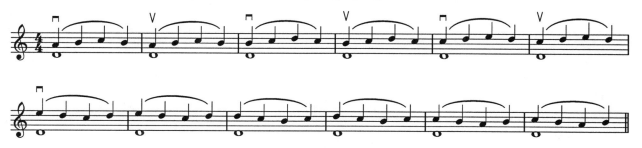

F. Double Stop Dexterity Exercises (thirds, sixths).

At first, stop after each double stop, reset fingers for next notes, then play. As security and coordination increase, decrease length of stops and gradually eliminate them. Strive for an equal sound between the two strings.

   Perhaps the best procedure is to use the lower note as the foundation to the upper note of the double stop. It should be set in place first with the upper note quickly falling into place. Using the correct spacing (measurement) from the lower to the upper note can assure good intonation. Keep fingers of the left hand positioned over the fingerboard. An excellent double stop dexterity exercise is to slur two and then four to a bow. It promotes strength in all fingers.

An interesting exercise is to play thirds and sixths on familiar pieces. This uses former pieces to learn new techniques.

Hot Cross Buns (sixths)

Pierrot's Door (thirds)

Twinkle in Double Stops (thirds and sixths)

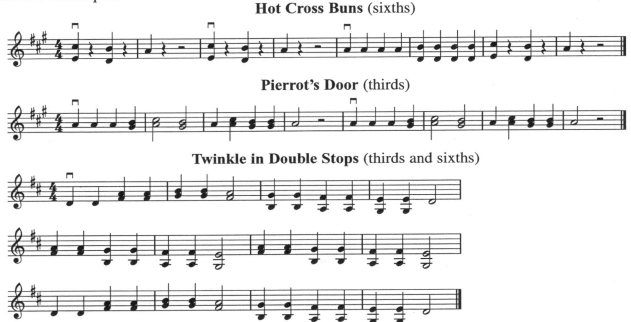

G. Shifting Octaves

The first finger serves as a guide in establishing the new position, whether ascending or descending. The distance between first and fourth fingers becomes smaller when shifting upward. When changing positions, keep the bow moving but release weight on bow and fingers to avoid a glissando sound.

144

H. Double Stop Shifting (thirds)

Double stop shifting is the same principle as for single notes. The entire hand moves up as a unit. The first and third fingers and bow release pressure on strings when sliding up (or down). The first finger and thumb lead the way when shifting down.

I. Double Stop Shifting (sixths)

Same principles of shifting as in thirds. The first finger and thumb together with the hand move as a unit going up and first finger and thumb lead the way coming down.

III. DOUBLE STOP EXCERPTS FROM SUZUKI REPERTOIRE
(How to Practice Exercises)

A. Playing More Advanced Pieces.

As the repertoire advances, double stop passages occur that contain several kinds of techniques of articulations, string crossings and a variety of bowings and finger patterns. Through this maintain a good tone quality on both strings. For example, several of these techniques appear in the following passage:

Concerto No. 2, Third Movement (Volume 4) - Seitz

Practice at a slow $\frac{6}{8}$ (six beats to a measure) with accents, separate and slurred staccato bowings and double stops on open strings. Also, concentrate on proper weight and tone quality on all strings. In the three-note chord, aim bow at middle note with all three notes played together. When all is going well and under control, play as written at slow $\frac{6}{8}$ tempo; (two beats to a measure); then gradually increase to the tempo of the piece. The best part of the bow to play this passage is just below the middle. Proper bowing and execution of accents and staccatos are explained in detail in Chapter 9.

B. Extensive Double Stop Playing.

Concerto No. 5, Third Movement - Seitz

This passage contains twenty-five consecutive measures of double stops. A similar approach can be used as in Section A. First practice on open strings concentrating on bowings and articulations (détaché and staccato), and a balance of tones between the strings. Play just below the middle of the bow and close to the fingerboard (*mf*) with equal sound on both strings. Slow practice, at first, allows the mind to focus on proper bowing. Increase tempo as proficiency develops to where the bowings are working very well. Now play passage as written in the piece slowly, then gradually increase tempo. Practicing complex passages such as the one illustrated should be simplified so that a student can concentrate on the basic structure. Repeating this practice passage in outline form several times brings the bowings into a semi-memorized state with correct execution. Playing these measures with bow and left hand together is the next step. With this approach, everything is brought under control.

IV. PLAYING CHORDS

A. Broken Chords (Three notes)

The lower and middle notes are played together before the beat with the value equal to a grace note. The bow then rotates into the middle and upper notes with the middle one played in both cases. These are played on the beat. Bow weight is placed on the middle note which is the center of the chord. This makes it easier to angle from the lower to the upper notes. The forearm and elbow are the primary movements that lead the bow arm from the lower to the upper notes in an arc-like motion. Draw the bow slowly on bottom notes and faster with more bow on the top notes.

Example: Concerto No. 2, Third Movement (Volume 4) - Seitz (last four measures)

Keep the first finger (B) on the string between chords.

B. Broken Chords (four notes)

The lower two notes are played together before the beat and then over to the top two notes which are played together on the beat. The bow arm makes an arc-like movement with the forearm and elbow dropping and leading the way which frees the shoulder from any tight feeling or tension. The upper arm will move slightly backward. Weight into the bow comes from the entire arm into the middle fingers of the bow hold.

C. Unbroken Chords (three notes)

Three-note unbroken chords are played by dropping the bow on the strings aiming at the center of the chord, which is the middle note. Enough weight should be used so that the bow touches the outer strings causing all three strings to be played together. The basic movement comes from the forearm and elbow although the entire arm is involved. A higher drop will produce a more percussive sound. Sometimes this effect is desired. To produce a series of chords with a smooth, consistent sound, keep the bow closer to the strings and fingerboard where the strings are more flexible and at a more even level. For a louder sound, play closer to the bridge with more arm weight. The best place to play chords is just below the middle of the bow. Too close to the frog will create a crushed and harsh quality since this is the heaviest part of the bow. Consecutive three-note unbroken chords are usually played with down bow strokes with the arm moving in small circles going from chord to chord (lift and reset motion ⊓⊓).

Example: Caprice No. 24 (Variation 8) - Paganini

Note: Playing chords often results in a forced bow stroke producing a scratchy tone quality. This is caused by a tense arm weight placed into the first and second fingers of the bow hold which comes from a tight shoulder and upper arm. Psychologically, seeing a three or four-note chord to be played in one stroke does create a tense feeling which in turn causes excessive weight. To create a resonant sound, the natural weight of the arm should go directly into the center of the bow hold (second and third with the aid of the fourth finger). To obtain this feeling, practice playing chords with the first finger raised slightly off the bow. Chord playing requires more bow and arm weight than single notes, but only enough bow and weight to achieve a good tone quality. After the proper weight and tone quality are obtained, place first finger on the bow which will supply some weight and help support and control the bow movement.

V. PLAYING ARPEGGIOS WITH DOUBLE STOP FINGERINGS

Playing arpeggios requires special bowing and left hand techniques. In slurred arpeggios across three or four strings, the bow makes a smooth circular movement both from bottom to upper strings and from top to lower strings. Do not seek a plateau for each string, but gauge the speed and level of the bow arm for a smooth and curved movement. The forearm and elbow lead the way when crossing to upper strings. The hand leads the way going from upper to lower strings. The elbow will come up slightly, but should continue to remain fairly low. Use a double stop approach by setting the left fingers in place quickly before each arpeggio.

Listed below are examples of exercises preparing arpeggio passages:
1. Without the bow, practice double stop settings of left fingers for each arpeggio.
2. Bow each double stop setting with an arc-like movement when crossing strings.
3. Proceed to play etude as written.

Preparing Etude by Tartini

Apply these arc-like bowings and left hand double stop techniques when preparing this etude.

ETUDE

G. TARTINI

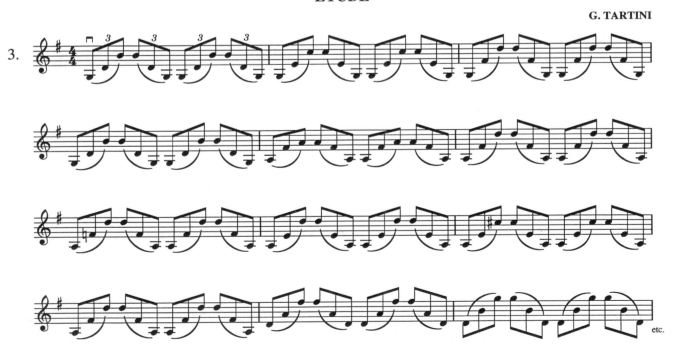

148

CHAPTER 11
PRIVATE STUDIO AND CLASSROOM
STRING TEACHING PROGRAMS: ALTERNATIVES

I.   INTRODUCTION: SUGGESTIONS FOR WAYS TO DESIGN A PEDAGOGY 150

II.   TEACHING AND READING PROGRAMS IN SUZUKI VOLUMES 1, 2............................150

III. EXAMPLES OF STRING METHOD BOOKS 155

IV.   THE USE OF REVIEW AND REFINE TO ACCELERATE TECHNICAL
      AND MUSICAL GROWTH (FOR PRIVATE OR CLASS INSTRUCTION) 156

CHAPTER 11
PRIVATE STUDIO AND CLASSROOM
STRING TEACHING PROGRAMS: ALTERNATIVES

I. INTRODUCTION: SUGGESTIONS FOR WAYS TO DESIGN A PEDAGOGY

All string teachers must design a pedagogy and adapt it to their own teaching style, philosophy and situation. Some may select one particular approach or method of teaching and perhaps, make modifications. Others may use an eclectic approach; that is, extracting ideas from many different sources and consolidating them into a method that is appropriate to their way of teaching.

Although this study applies many principles of Suzuki, it also refers to instructional principles and techniques from renowned pedagogues such as Dalcroze, Ševčik, Schradieck, Flesch, Galamian, Applebaum, Rolland and Havas. The primary focus of this text is on structuring an approach to teaching from beginning through intermediate levels using this eclectic format. It is designed for both private studio and classroom string teachers.

An effective instructional format must have an interesting and appropriate teaching repertoire. As an example, Suzuki established a very impressive philosophy and pedagogy combined with a carefully selected repertoire. The pieces have musical appeal to young players and build technical and musical skills sequentially. He also composed and arranged pieces containing a particular technique and inserted these into the collection to keep the technical and musical skills progressing in logical order. When a problem would arise, he used the mini-etude to work it out. This helps the student focus on and solve this awkward spot, gain a new skill and perform the entire piece with confidence. The outcome: a new playing facility and a new piece added to the general playing repertoire. Reviewing and refining previous pieces lead to mastery. The result: an extremely successful teaching and learning approach.

In summary, the important issues to consider when designing a way of teaching is to know *what* to teach, *when* to teach it and *how* to teach it. As previously stated, an interesting and sequential repertoire is at the center of this pedagogy. Related exercises, scales and etudes used in conjunction with this repertoire create a well conceived and productive integration of teaching material. When and how to develop playing skills (a pedagogy) using this collection of material is explained in preceding chapters.

II. TEACHING AND READING PROGRAMS IN SUZUKI VOLUMES 1 AND 2
A. Example of a Teaching and Reading Program While in Volume 1
Suggested for ages eight and older. For private studio and classroom strings (four stages):

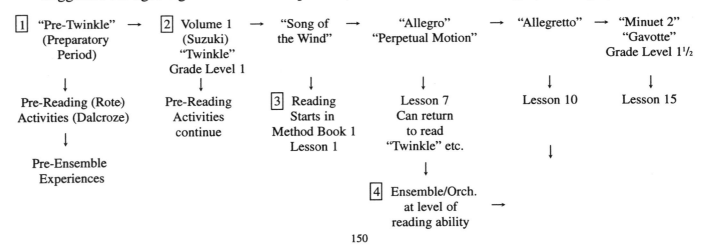

Refer to Chapter 9 for a detailed pre-reading and note-reading plan. The above program is adjustable. Some teachers may delay reading until "Minuet 1" instead of "Song of the Wind." The time to begin reading is at the discretion of the teacher, the playing ability and age of the student.

B. Example of a Teaching and Reading Program Upon Completion of Volume 1.

Primarily for private studio string teaching four stages:

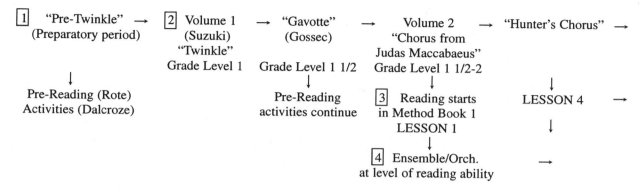

C. An Explanation of the Four Stages of Development

Stage 1: Rote Teaching. Dalcroze Eurhythmics. Beginning Playing Techniques.

Starting with the "pre-Twinkle" songs, the student is taught by rote to establish playing posture, left hand and proper bowing movements. Clapping, marching, singing the rhythm and melody of each song is encouraged as this not only develops intrinsic aural and rhythmic skills, but also teaches the songs. Coordinating internal eurhythmic skills with physical playing skills creates a foundation for the beginning string player. The Dalcroze activities will help to accomplish this objective. Students begin to relate these early pieces to fingering notes and intervals on the violin as well as proper bowing rhythmic movements in the bow arm.

Pizzicato playing scale patterns of three-four notes outlines the short eight-measure familiar songs (e.g. "Mary Had a Little Lamb," etc.). This is practiced on the A and then the E string. The next step is to pluck the complete octave (A major scale). The student, in the meantime, is exercising bowing actions of quarter notes and "Twinkle" rhythms with silent bowing. Both hands are now prepared to play these scale patterns, the A major scale, the simple songs and "Twinkle" rhythms.

An early pre-ensemble experience can be achieved with second and third parts and a piano accompaniment to the preparatory songs (e.g. "Mary Had a Little Lamb," "Hot Cross Buns," etc.). The parts are included in Chapter 1.

Another interesting pre-ensemble activity is to play a scale in canon style and in contrary motion; also, "Partner Songs" which consist of two different songs with the same keys, tonality and measures played at the same time. In a private lesson, the teacher plays one part and the student the other part. In a class, parts can be divided between two groups. These activities gradually develop students to become independent players concentrating on their own part, keeping strict time and listening and blending with another part. These are important ensemble and orchestral playing qualities which can be played by rote.

CANON STYLE

Part 1 using same rhythm in both parts

Part 1 using two different rhythms

CONTRARY MOTION

Using same rhythm

Using different rhythms

Note: A canon is a musical form in the style of strict imitation with the second part repeating exactly what the first part played, usually starting in the second measure.

"Partner Songs." These are two different songs played at the same time. Both songs must be compatible as to the key, meter, harmony and number of measures. These are difficult to find but at this early stage "Twinkle" and "May Song" present this ensemble-type experience in an interesting way. As soon as the last measure has been completed, the songs are immediately repeated but the parts are exchanged. The "Twinkle" part now plays "May Song."

Stage 2: Pre-Reading Ensemble Experiences Continued.

To this point, the student, by rote, has established a daily review and refine practice routine of rhythms, bowings and articulation on the A major scale with basic techniques of left hand and bowing becoming secure and flexible. Rote playing of Volume 1 pieces are increasing. The student is now ready for some ensemble-type experiences. Preparation for this started with some pre-ensemble activities illustrated in Stage 1. Stage 2 brings the student to a higher level by playing the solo part with piano and string orchestra accompaniment. Listed below are Suzuki pieces that have the first violin (solo part) played by the student by rote with the accompanying parts played by the teacher or older students who have reading abilities. Continue this experience when reading develops.

(a) *Duets for Violins* (Second and First Parts consist of selected pieces from the Suzuki Violin School, Volumes 1, 2, 3). Composed by Suzuki, Summy-Birchard Inc., distributed by Warner Bros. Publications,

Miami, Florida, 1971).

(b) *String Orchestra Accompaniments* (to solos in Volumes 1, 2). Arranged by Paul Simmons. Selected and edited by John Kendall. Summy-Birchard Inc., 1974. (Distributed by Warner Bros. Publications, Miami, Florida, 1974).

Stage 3: Coordinating Suzuki Repertoire with String Method Books. Establishing a Reading Program.

The string method books are designed for both private studio as well as classroom strings and are an important part of a string teacher's pedagogy. These introduce and explain notes, rhythms, fingerings, keys, articulations, positions and bowings through a series of scales, exercises, pieces and etudes. All of this is presented in an easy-to-read and understandable format. Another way to develop reading ability is to return to "Twinkle" and other previously studied pieces which were learned by rote and have the student read the music. *Quick Steps to Note Reading* (by J. Frederick Müller, Harold W. Rusch, Lorraine Fink) is a four-volume series and an excellent source in developing note reading. It combines scales, exercises, short pieces, and pieces from the Suzuki volumes. Piano accompaniments are included in selected repertoire. These move along at a slightly faster rate than the traditional string method book. It is especially designed for rote-trained students who are very proficient players and are beginning to read notation.

Reading should be delayed until basic left hand and bow techniques are secure. Improper playing actions of left hand and/or bowing can result if the foundation is not well-established. The teacher should determine what is the best playing and age level students should reach before starting a reading program.

Stage 4: An Example of Coordinating Suzuki Volumes 1 and 2 with Method Books, String Ensemble and Orchestra Repertoire.

(a) Listed below is an example of coordinating the playing proficiency level of Volumes 1 and 2 solo repertoire to that of the majority of string method books and string ensemble pieces. Keys, range, bowings, rhythms all match.

Suzuki Repertoire Volume 1	Reading/Playing Ability Lessons in Method Book 1	Same Level String Ensemble Repertoire
"Lightly Row" through "Etude"	Lessons 8-15	*Easy Pieces for String Ensemble* by Jack Pernecky (M.M. Cole) 20 Pieces (Schop, Purcell, Couperin, Corelli, Bach, Haydn, Mozart, Pachelbel, Stravinsky).
"Minuet 1"	Lessons 10-15	*Learn to Play in Orchestra* (strings) by Ralph Matesky (Alfred). 28 Pieces (Corelli, Haydn, Bach, Beethoven, Bartok).
"Minuet 2"	Lessons 14-16	*Two Pieces for Young Strings* by K. Beecher (Shawnee Press)
"Minuet 3"	Lesson 17	*Music for Young Strings,* arr. A. Spatz (Shawnee Press)
Suzuki Repertoire Volume 2	Reading/Playing Ability Lessons in Method Book 2	Same Level String Ensemble Repertoire
"Hunter's Chorus"	Lesson 7	*Especially for Strings* by Robert Frost (Kjos). 20 Pieces (Handel, Scheidt, Christmas Carols)
"Bourrée"	Lesson 10	*Fiddler's Square Dance,* arr. James McLeod (Kjos)
"Gavotte"	Lesson 11	*Dance of the Tumblers from "Snow Maiden"* (Rimsky-Korsakoff) arr. Sandra Dackow (Luck's)

Example: Students who learn by rote through "Minuet I" (Volume 1) may have the playing ability to learn to read through Lesson 15 in the string method book 1 plus a variety of string ensemble and orchestra music.

(b) Suzuki Repertoire from Volumes 1, 2 arranged for ensembles:

(1) *String Quartets for Beginning Ensembles, Volume 1* (Selections from Suzuki Volume 1, arranged for string quartet). Arranged by Joseph Knaus, Summy-Birchard Inc., distributed by Warner Bros. Publications, Miami, Florida, 1990.

(2) *String Orchestra Accompaniments* (to pieces in Volumes 1 and 2). Arranged by Paul Simmons, selected and edited by John Kendall. Summy-Birchard Inc., distributed by Warner Bros. Publications, Miami, Florida, 1974.

III. EXAMPLES OF STRING METHOD BOOKS.

These assist in developing reading and playing abilities and can be coordinated with Suzuki and ensemble repertoire. They can be used for private studio and classroom strings.

Title	Author	Publisher
Action with Strings	Robert Klotman	Southern
All for Strings (Bks. 1, 2)	Gerald Anderson & Robert Frost	Kjos
Applebaum String Method (Bks. 1, 2, 3)	Samuel Applebaum	Warner Bros.
Belwin String Builder (Bks. 1, 2, 3)	Samuel Applebaum	Warner Bros.
Bornoff's Finger Patterns	George Bornoff	Big 3
Essential Elements (Bks. 1, 2)	Michael Allen, Robert Gillespie, Pamela Tellejohn Hayes	Hal Leonard
Growing with Strings (Bks. 1, 2)	Jack Pernecky	M.M. Cole
Learn to Play an Instrument (Bks. 1, 2)	Ralph Matesky & Ardelle Womack	Alfred
Learning Unlimited String Program (Bks. 1, 2)	Thomas Wisniewski & John Higgins	Hal Leonard
Müller-Rusch String Method (Bks. 1, 2, 3, 4, 5)	J. Frederick Müller, Harold Rusch	Kjos
Quick Steps to Note Reading	J. Frederick Müller, Harold Rusch, Lorraine Fink	Kjos
Strictly Strings (Bks. 1, 2, 3)	Jacquelyn Dillon, James Kjelland, John O'Reilly	Highland/Etling
String Class Method (Bks. 1, 2, 3)	Forest Etling	Etling
String Class Method (Bks. 1, 2)	Merle Isaac	M.M. Cole
Young Strings in Action (Bks. 1, 2)	Sheila Johnson	Boosey & Hawkes

The content of *String Method,* Books 1-6 is listed in Chapter 4: Guidelines in Determining Grade Levels.

Recordings are one of Suzuki's primary teaching and learning mediums. These develop musical sensitivity in the young student in memory recall and musical alertness of melodies, rhythms, articulations, styles of the repertoire that soon will be studied. Cassettes and compact discs are available for many of the string method books. Exercises, scales and short pieces are played as they appear in the lessons. Each one has a rhythm and/or a harmonized accompaniment.

Many publishers have sample cassette tapes of graded ensemble and orchestra music of all styles and periods. These give the teacher an opportunity to also hear the level of difficulty.

IV. THE USE OF REVIEW AND REFINE TO ACCELERATE TECHNICAL AND MUSICAL GROWTH (FOR PRIVATE OR CLASS INSTRUCTION)

This is one of Suzuki's teaching principles that has great merit. Repetition leads to security and provides a way to achieve mastery. For instance, repeating and refining rhythms, bowings, dynamics, tempos, articulations on scales, etudes or familiar pieces (e.g. "Twinkle" Variations) can be studied daily in a student's practice schedule or in class with all students playing and learning together. With techniques working well, reviewing and refining earlier pieces for musical expression and dynamics is a most desirable objective.

As an example, while working on a new piece (e.g. "Allegretto" Volume 1), the following bowings, rhythms and articulations from earlier pieces can be refined on scales or used as a "Twinkle" variation. To augment the learning, transfer the scale and variations to different strings (e.g. A/E, D/A, G/D). Study the movements of fingers of left hand and wrist, forearm, elbow and upper arm on each bowing.

Use the mental and physical approach by concentrating on tension-free, well-coordinated actions of both hands. A solid playing foundation develops.

Earlier Pieces	Review Bowings on Scales Extracted from These Pieces
Pre-Twinkle songs, "Twinkle"	Staccato ♩ ♩ ♩ ♩ ‖ ♫ ♫ ‖
Pre-Twinkle songs, "Twinkle", "Lightly Row"	Détaché ♩ ♩ ♩ ♩ ‖ ♫♫ ♩ ‖ ♫♫♫ ‖ ♫ ♩ ‖
"Lightly Row"	Bow Division ♩ ♩ ♩ ‖
"May Song"	Martelé ♩ ♩ ♩ ♩ ‖ Dotted Notes ♩. ♪♩. ♪ ‖
"Allegretto" (new piece)	Accent ♫♫♫ ‖

When playing with other students, play these bowings in unison. Also, in two-three-four part canon style and two-part contrary motion for ensemble experiences.

CHAPTER 12
KEEPING INTEREST ALIVE
(Motivating Students)

I.   GETTING AN INTERESTING START
     Eurhythmic Activities in "pre-Twinkle" (Preparatory) Period 159

II. SEQUENTIAL LEARNING
     Involving Students in the Learning Process 159

III. KNOWING HOW TO PRACTICE
     Teaching Students to Become Effective "Practicers" 159

IV. KNOWING WHAT TO PRACTICE
     Relating Repertoire and Technical Studies 160

V.   MAKING MUSIC WITH OTHERS WITH GROUP INSTRUCTION
     Sharing Ideas with Others 160

VI. SELECTING INTERESTING MUSIC
     Use of Interesting Supplementary Music 161

VII. INFORMAL AND FORMAL RECITALS 161

VIII. PARENTAL SUPPORT 161

IX. ENSEMBLE PLAYING 161

CHAPTER 12
KEEPING INTEREST ALIVE
(Motivating Students)

There are many different reasons why students study an instrument: curiosity, urging and encouragement by parents, fascination for a particular instrument, socialization, love of making music. Whatever the reason, it is the teacher's responsibility to move this forward into an exciting musical and educational experience. The teacher's challenge is to have the student attain the maximum level of playing proficiency in a reasonable period of time which will in turn keep the interest at a high level. Therefore, it is essential that the approach to teaching contain interesting and meaningful repertoire and activities taught in a logical, easy to understand and productive way.

Listed below are suggestions which can motivate learning.

I. GETTING AN INTERESTING START.

This is an important period of time for both student and teacher. The beginning student is looking forward to an exciting experience. The teacher must maintain this enthusiasm while developing highly technical and complex skills.

An enjoyable and creative beginning stage is recommended, such as the Dalcroze activities program suggested in the "pre-Twinkle" (preparatory period). Marching and clapping (meter) while singing the melody (rhythm, pitch) to familiar songs is fun to do. Students keep active by singing, moving and playing musical games with others in class and at home with the family. Students develop an internal feeling of aural and rhythmic sensitivity which is directly applied to the music to be played. These concepts are then transferred to the teaching of left hand and bowing techniques. Both student and teacher benefit from these preparatory period activities.

II. SEQUENTIAL LEARNING.

Each technique must be explained and demonstrated in logical sequence and in simple terms that are appropriate to the age and ability of the student. The young player becomes directly involved by following this step-by-step explanation and demonstration by the teacher, and repeats back to the teacher that which was presented. This is a form of role playing. The student becomes the teacher and through this mental and physical process becomes actively involved. During the young player's private lesson, the teacher can intentionally do something incorrectly to test the student's understanding and alertness. This checks the accuracy of the learner's grasp of the teaching approach. It also establishes a model of how to practice by going through a verbal explanation (mental) and applying it to the instrument (physical). Avoid skipping an essential technique which serves as a prerequisite. This will often delay progress and interrupt the sequential line of development. Sequential teaching is an extremely important part of the learning process. Problem solving, analytical thinking and reasoning, interrelating ideas, communication skills are the educational values gained by the student from this type of instruction.

III. KNOWING HOW TO PRACTICE.

Understanding how to practice instills confidence in a student and accelerates progress. A primary function of the teacher is to clearly explain practice procedures. When the student is able to effectively manage the practice routine, progress is visible and the incentive to practice is increased. With more practice comes greater progress.

It is also important to know what to practice. If a scale is to be used in the daily practice schedule, the teacher must explain what to practice on the scale, and how to practice it. If studying a certain articulation (e.g. martelé), show what part of the bow arm to use, what parts of the bow arm are involved, how is it accented and how much bow to use. This is explained and demonstrated in turn by the student. The same procedure is used when working out technical problems in the repertoire by using mini-exercises and etudes.

At lesson time, the teacher may ask the students to give an explanation and demonstration of how they practiced a new piece during the past week and how the problems were worked out using this inter-related material. This is similar to a classroom teacher asking students to give a report of their homework to see if they obtained the proper information or to get their interpretation of a reading assignment. Over a period of time, the student becomes an excellent and productive "practicer." Progress is enhanced and motivation is increased.

There is a familiar saying that illustrates this teaching style:

> "Tell me and I will forget,
> Show me and I may remember,
> Involve me and I will learn."

IV. KNOWING WHAT TO PRACTICE.

Students must recognize the need to practice scales, exercises and etudes as a means to achieve the skills to perform the music effectively. These technical studies are essential. Each has a particular purpose and is used in special ways. From the very beginning, the teacher structures the lesson to show how to apply and relate these studies to the repertoire. Teaching a student how and what to practice is an integral part of the lesson.

How does one assemble this kind of teaching material? As previously stated, the core of this material is an interesting collection of sequentially organized pieces. These are graded according to levels of difficulty. As each piece presents technical and musical problems, and certain skills that need to be emphasized, the supporting scale, exercise, mini-exercise and etude assist in working out the problems and strengthening the general playing skills. These should also be selected for sequential order to match the keys, range, rhythms and bowings of the pieces. Once these problems and skills are worked out, the piece is added to the daily review and refine practice schedule to achieve technical and musical mastery.

With this teaching and practice "curriculum" of everything working together in logical order, the student's interest in practicing will be highly motivated because it all makes sense and produces positive results.

V. MAKING MUSIC WITH OTHERS WITH GROUP INSTRUCTION.

It is an enjoyable experience to work together as a unit and study special techniques with friends. The students learn from each other and share their accomplishments as well as their problems. Those who need to strengthen a weak area or learn a new technique can quickly work this out with the group — a cooperative learning environment. Perhaps the most inspiring experience is contributing to a larger, more dynamic sound while improving one's own techniques and musicianship. This activity encourages practice because each student is challenged to play well when performing with others.

1. Various types of instruction can be used in group teaching. The teacher can have the group play special rhythms, bowings and articulations on scales, checking to see if everyone is performing these correctly. For instance, if some of the students are not executing the martelé stroke properly, the teacher can

explain and demonstrate this technique or may ask a student who performs it well to explain and demonstrate. This type of review is a quick way to reinforce the performance of this bowing to the entire group. When all students are playing this stroke properly, move it into an interesting ensemble-type experience. Divide the class into two or three sections to play an octave scale using the form of a canon with everyone executing the martelé bowing. (Chapter 11 explains this form). Different volume levels and dynamics can also be studied.

2. Study an etude together emphasizing string crossings, finger dexterity and bowings (e.g. lift and reset, staccato, etc.). Teaching these playing skills to a group often saves private lesson time. Those who are slower in understanding can observe others who are doing well.

3. Study new repertoire together. Form a group of students who are working on the same piece(s). The scale and exercises would be used on special problems or new techniques that need to be reinforced within these piece(s). Students are taught and learn together. This saves teaching new pieces and techniques at private lesson time. Special problems and individual progress can be studied at private lessons.

4. Finally, review and refine previous pieces by studying nuances, dynamics, tempos, phrasing and style by making music together. A piano accompaniment and/or a second part played by older students or the teacher creates a delightful ensemble experience.

VI. SELECTING INTERESTING MUSIC.

Semi-classical, familiar folk songs, ethnic songs, hoe downs (an excellent bowing, rhythm, string crossing study) can stimulate interest and add variety to the musical dimensions. These can be inserted and sequenced within the regular Suzuki repertoire. The technical style of the Hoe Down is similar to an etude and, on occasion, can serve as a substitute.

VII. INFORMAL AND FORMAL RECITALS.

Solo recitals can be scheduled regularly with parents and friends attending and supporting the young players. With a daily practice routine and a repertoire class reviewing and refining older pieces, the students have a performance repertoire readily available. Further polishing the selected solo piece in a private lesson would lead to a very presentable solo performance. This is a highly motivating event.

VIII. PARENTAL SUPPORT.

This is the key to success for young students in whatever subject is being studied. Attending lessons, allocating daily practice time, attending recitals and concerts, acknowledging accomplishments, taking them to concerts, listening to musical recordings at home — all display interest and support. Joining a parent group to support the teacher and music program is a way to help create an environment for musical learning.

IX. ENSEMBLE PLAYING.

This is undoubtedly a goal that every young student would like to reach — to be an excellent ensemble and orchestra player. It is a challenge for the teacher to build a student's playing technique and note reading ability in order to be prepared for ensemble and orchestra playing.

The private teacher has an excellent opportunity to cultivate the essentials for ensemble playing. The beginning rote period can be extended according to the age and playing ability of the student. A three-year-old can be a pretty good player in two-and-a-half to three years at which time reading can be introduced. In cases where the teacher wants to concentrate on technical and musical development through an extensive rote period, note reading can be delayed until the completion of Volume 1 or 2.

The classroom string teacher who starts students in the third or fourth grade has a much shorter period of time to develop both individual playing and reading proficiencies. Usually, after a year of class instruction, the student has been note reading from the string method book and has the ability to read easy orchestra music.

In either case, both the private and classroom string teacher can develop individual playing skills as well as prepare orchestra players at the same time. Obviously, the more advanced players will progress faster in learning notation. Classroom string teachers who give instruction to groups of students often suggest additional instruction from a private teacher to achieve a faster rate of technical and musical growth.

Details of a curriculum for both types of programs (private and string class) are included in Chapter 11.

CHAPTER 13
LEARNING MUSIC THROUGH MUSICAL FORM

I.   INTRODUCTION 164

II.   EXAMPLE FROM VOLUME 1 "ALLEGRO," FORM AABA 164

III. EXAMPLE FROM VOLUME 2 "BOURRÉE," FORM AABA'BA' 165

IV.   EXAMPLES OF FORM IN SELECTED PIECES, VOLUMES 1, 2 AND 3 167

V.   BENEFITS OF USING FORM IN ROTE TEACHING ("pre-Twinkle," Volume 1) 167

VI.   SUGGESTIONS WHEN PREPARING TO STUDY A NEW PIECES (Volume 2, etc.)...........167

CHAPTER 13
LEARNING MUSIC THROUGH MUSICAL FORM

I. INTRODUCTION

Playing a new piece in its entirety over and over again hoping eventually to perform it well does not always bring satisfactory results or accomplish what each piece has to offer technically and musically. Learning reaches its optimum level when it is well organized and the piece is studied through a step-by-step process, and then unified. For instance, most of the pieces in Volume 1 are written in four-measure phrases or eight-measure sentences. When playing through a new piece, a student spots problem areas and uses special exercises and scales to achieve security and control of the technique. These trouble spots are usually within a measure or two. After these are worked out, the entire phrase (four measures) or sentence (eight measures) is played to work the former problem into a complete musical thought. It is similar to reading a text book. When a strange word appears, it is defined and clarified by referring to a dictionary, then the entire sentence or paragraph is read with greater meaning.

Identifying parts within a musical form:

A. Phrase There are many different lengths to a phrase. However, the typical phrase is four measures long ending with a half cadence or a full cadence. Many of the pieces in Volume 1 (especially the shorter ones) are structured in four-measure units.

B. Sentence A sentence consists of two four-measure phrases and ends with a complete cadence. The second phrase completes the musical thought of the first phrase. A complete musical thought can also extend to eight measures which appears in longer pieces.

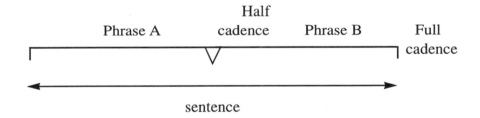

II. EXAMPLE FROM VOLUME 1 "ALLEGRO," FORM AABA.

This piece consists of sixteen measures or four phrases (AABA; 4+4+4+4 measures). Examining the musical structure, it actually consists of only two different phrases (AB; 4+4 measures). The practice procedure would be: (1) working out problem areas with mini-exercises and scales in each of the two phrases (e.g. string crossings, rhythm patterns, articulations); (2) when these are functioning well, play the entire phrase; (3) then join the two different phrases (AB); finally, play the entire piece.

When playing through the entire piece, select a slow to moderate tempo guiding both hands mentally and physically through each phrase. As security is achieved, increase to tempo indicated in the piece. The student has an intelligent and a semi-memorized grasp of the contents of each phrase and how each is related. Identifying phrases that are related saves practice time in learning the entire piece.

ALLEGRO
Shinichi Suzuki

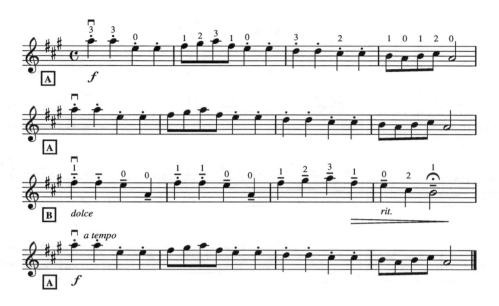

III. EXAMPLE FROM VOLUME 2 "BOURRÉE," FORM AABA′BA′

As the student advances, the pieces become longer and more complex. In "Bourrée," the form is AABA′BA′ with each section consisting of eight measures (a sentence). The A′ sentence contains a slight variation from the A sentence. When analyzing this piece, one can see only three different sections with two almost identical. With this type of analysis, this longer piece can be simplified and learned at a quicker pace.

Apply a four-step approach:

1. Study technical problems in each sentence with mini-exercises and scales.

2. When this is accomplished, practice the entire sentence to see how this comes together. Play each sentence several times to gain a smooth, secure performance. By this time, each sentence is almost memorized.

3. Proceed to tie sentences together (e.g. AAB; ABA′; A′BA′) or (e.g. AA; BA′; BA′).

4. Then play the entire piece.

A well-conceived plan can make learning a new piece easier, quicker and provide a technical and musical understanding of the entire work.

BOURRÉE

G.F. HANDEL

IV. EXAMPLES OF FORM IN SELECTED PIECES, VOLUMES 1, 2 AND 3

A. Volume 1.

Listed below are pieces from this Volume identifying forms and the number of measures in each phrase or sentence.

"Lightly Row" AA'BA' (4+4+4+4 measures; three different phrases) "Go Tell Aunt Rhody" ABA (4+4+4 measures; two different phrases) "O Come Little Children" AABC (4+4+4+4 measures; three different phrases) "Perpetual Motion" ABCA (4+4+4+4 measures; three different phrases) "Minuet 2" AA'BCA' (8+8+8+8+8 measures; four different sentences).

B. Volume 2.

"Chorus from 'Judas Maccabaeus'" (G.F. Handel) ABA (8+8+8 measures; two different sentences) "Long, Long Ago" (T.H. Bayly) 2 sections: Moderato AA BA (4+4+4+4 measures, three different phrases; variation AA'BA', three different phrases).

C. Volume 3

"Gavotte" (P. Martini) ABACADAEAFA (Each 8 measures; 6 same and 5 different sentences).

V. BENEFITS OF USING FORM IN ROTE TEACHING ("pre-Twinkle," Volume 1)

The phrase and sentence method of teaching is an excellent approach when teaching by rote. The student listens to the recording to obtain aural and rhythmic concepts of the music as well as the general structure. Repetition of the melodic line is recognized. At lesson time when presenting a new piece, "Go Tell Aunt Rhody" for instance, the teacher plays the whole piece and explains that there are three parts. The first and third are the same, the middle or second part is different. The teacher then plays the first part (phrase), stops; plays the second part (phrase), stops; then plays the third part (phrase) which is the same as the first phrase. By listening to the recording and the teacher's demonstration and explanation, the young student has a fairly good idea of the structure and content of the piece. Even teaching two measures at a time or a half phrase makes musical sense; then the second half to complete the phrase. The student sees the balance between the two phrases. Learning is increased if presented in an organized and logical manner.

VI. SUGGESTIONS WHEN PREPARING TO STUDY A NEW PIECE
(Volume 2, etc., when note reading has been developed)

1. Play the entire new piece two-three times slower than tempo (but in strict time) to obtain a general understanding of the content and structure, and to identify the problems. It is suggested that new pieces be slightly more difficult than the previous ones. If the new piece contains many problems and is too challenging, a greater period of time and patience is needed to overcome the many difficult parts which may discourage the student and delay progress. Sequential development is extremely important and will bring better and quicker results.

2. Extract awkward/problem areas which can be studied with mini-exercises, scales, etudes.

3. Identify repeated phrases and sentences. Know the form of the piece.

4. When problem spots have been worked out, practice these in the form of phrases and sentences.

5. Begin to study the entire piece combining phrases and sentences. Use slower tempo at first but keep a steady beat.

6. When all is going well, increase tempo. However, keep practicing the problem spots (often newer techniques) on scales and etudes to increase proficiency.

CHAPTER 14
CREATING AN EFFECTIVE PEDAGOGY

I.   IDENTIFYING CONTENTS OF AN EFFECTIVE APPROACH TO TEACHING.................169

II.   HOW THIS TEXT, *TEACHING THE FUNDAMENTALS OF VIOLIN PLAYING*
        WAS DEVELOPED..169

III.   SCHOOLS OF PEDAGOGY: EXAMPLES OF INFLUENCES ON THIS TEXT
        Piaget, Schradieck, Ševčik, Galamian, Alexander, Havas, Rolland, Suzuki, Flesch. 169

CHAPTER 14
CREATING AN EFFECTIVE PEDAGOGY

I. IDENTIFYING CONTENTS OF AN EFFECTIVE APPROACH TO TEACHING

As teachers we need to have a thorough knowledge of the philosophical, psychological and sociological as well as the pedagogical aspects of learning. There must be an understanding of how students learn, what kind of learning occurs at particular age levels and the best way to introduce a new idea to attract mental attention. Also, what kind of support encourages development, what kind of teaching material to use and how to use and present this material. As previously stated, knowing what to teach, how to teach and when to teach each technical and musical skill is essential when creating a productive pedagogy. Where does one obtain all this knowledge in order to become a fine teacher? It requires a thorough study of the learning process of children and an approach to teaching that is interesting, motivating, sequential and within their mental and physical capabilities. There may not be two teachers who teach exactly alike, but both may be very effective. However, there are basic instructional strategies that help to produce fine young players who not only achieve technical and musical skills, but cognitive skills as well; that is, the ability to create, analyze, relate, organize, express, communicate, think and reason critically. Suggestions on how to develop these essentials are included in this text.

II. HOW THIS TEXT, *TEACHING THE FUNDAMENTALS OF VIOLIN PLAYING,* WAS DEVELOPED

This text is based on a study of the philosophies and pedagogies of many prominent teachers, extensive research and personal teaching experiences. Some of these influences are listed in this next section. The most appropriate ideas from these sources have been modified by the author and placed into this teaching guide especially designed for students from the beginning through intermediate levels. This is the process every teacher must seriously consider when developing a pedagogy that is systematic, interesting, motivating and productive.

Teaching the way one has been taught may be sufficient if it has had satisfactory results. However, there are many resources available today to broaden and enrich teaching ideas which are applicable to all levels of playing such as attending string pedagogy classes and workshops, master classes, studying educational and child psychology and studying the development of cognitive skills which makes the student a better learner. These resources have also influenced the pedagogical ideas presented in this text.

The art of teaching is a creative and individualistic profession. Each string teacher must be thoroughly prepared to take the responsibility of enhancing the musical and technical abilities of students whether they are beginners or advanced players. Preparing oneself to be an effective teacher in any subject requires extensive study in many areas such as those previously listed.

III. SCHOOLS OF PEDAGOGY: EXAMPLES OF INFLUENCES ON THIS TEXT

Piaget, Jean. A Swiss psychologist and a specialist in child development who believed that the preschool child should be given the opportunity to develop sensory-motor functions to promote freedom to move and respond to games and music. These pre-school years are critical to a child's mental, social and emotional growth. Piaget's research and writing were centered in cognitive development of mental processes such as perceiving, remembering, believing and reasoning in children. Cognitive development is cumulative; that is, the understanding of a new experience grows out of what was learned from the previous one. This is a type of sequential and interrelated learning. Piaget was interested in the qualitative, not quantitative traits of development. It is not how much a child knows, but how the child has come to learn it. Product plus the process. Reasoning is the essence of intelligence.

Schradieck, Henry. Made important contributions by designing finger dexterity exercises in his technical books to develop correct finger movements, flexibility and even execution. These give strength and endurance to all fingers in all positions and are an excellent preparation for fast passages, runs and trills. These are to be practiced in all parts of the bow which emphasizes even tone quality throughout the bow. Also there are exercises in double stops, chord studies, scale studies. Although some of the exercises may be difficult for beginning students, these can be simplified and arranged for beginning through intermediate levels.

Ševčík, Otakar. Wrote scale studies from 1st position (one octave) through 7th position. Also, exercises in double stops (thirds through tenths), bowing techniques, articulation, shifting, trill studies and string crossing scales include all keys. Ideas can be arranged and simplified for beginning through intermediate levels.

Galamian, Ivan. A renowned pedagogue who expressed his teaching philosophy and ideas in *Principles of Violin Playing and Teaching*. Some of these teaching principles are directed at the beginning level and expand into the intermediate and advanced stages. His book is a practical guide on topics such as bowing and left hand techniques, shifting, intonation, articulation, double stop and chord playing. He emphasizes the use of a mental-physical correlation of mind and left hand and bowing actions when practicing. Slow practice is encouraged with a gradual increase in tempo over several days as security and accuracy develop.

Alexander, F. Matthias. A critic to any type of "inhibition"; that is, any restraint or repression. There must be tension-free movements in all physical actions. He explains how the mind and body work together. The two are not separate functions, but act cooperatively and simultaneously, each affecting the other. Coordinate, do not isolate physical movements when holding the instrument, bowing, vibrating, shifting, etc. There must be freedom of movement but all should be under control. He explains how to accomplish this in his writings. Most students begin with stiffness, tightness in left hand and bowing causing problems in intonation, finger dexterity, tone quality, flexibility in bowing and changing positions. These can be avoided if taught properly. The mind and body must be unified.

Havas, Kato. A violin teacher who adapted the Alexander techniques in her teaching. She translated the philosophical and psychological reasoning of Alexander into specific teaching principles of left hand and bow movements as applied to violin playing. She has been a great influence on Rolland and other leading string teachers.

Rolland, Paul. A professor of violin at the University of Illinois who applied the Alexander and Havas principles of tension-free playing in his approach to teaching. He developed a systematic study with explanations and illustrations on ways to eliminate unnecessary rigidity and excessive tension in order to obtain efficient, coordinated skills in left hand and bowing action. He developed special exercises such as tonality games (to establish proper left hand position, intonation, finger dexterity); motion games (to develop freedom of tension and coordinate bow arm movement when playing various types of bowings and articulations). Using experienced string specialists as consultants and studying ideas from outstanding pedagogues from the past and present, in addition to his own teaching experience, Rolland began to organize a unique approach.

During his period of research, he analyzed the teachings of Capet, Dounes, Flesch, Alexander, Polnauer, Hellebrandt, Havas, Suzuki. Born in Hungary, he marveled at the gypsies who played intricate folk songs learned by rote. He agreed with Suzuki that aural and rhythmic skills can be learned at an early age and serve as a foundation for musical and technical development. Rolland began a lab school for youngsters to try out his ideas and refine his pedagogical concepts. The result was a superb contribution to forming an approach to teaching.

Suzuki, Shinichi. The basic philosophy underlying his teaching is to enrich children's lives through music. The theory that every child has musical potential resulted in a pedagogy that not only develops musical abilities but also contributes to educational and personal growth. Critical thinking, organization and analytical abilities, discipline, creativity, cooperative learning and social interaction, enjoyment in achieving, motivation — all are essential to personal development. He felt that these human values could be instilled through a carefully designed approach when teaching music. Important parts of this pedagogy are the private lesson, the involvement of parents, working with other students in group lessons and motivating students to enjoy their learning. This psychological and sociological environment makes learning to play an instrument challenging and enjoyable. Suzuki's Violin School, Volumes 1 through 10 contain a collection of pieces arranged so that the student gradually develops playing skills through interesting repertoire. Students progress by working out problem areas with mini-exercises and special exercises, thereby adding new techniques: reviewing and refining previous pieces leads to mastering techniques and musicianship and provides the foundation for future pieces. Suzuki shared his teaching ideas in international workshops with young players illustrating his unique pedagogy. He has made a significant contribution to the philosophical, psychological and pedagogical aspects of teaching.

Flesch, Carl. Designed a unique scale system in all major and minor keys which includes single notes, chromatics, thirds, sixths, octaves, tenths, harmonics. It covers 1st through advanced positions. Various bowings and rhythms are included. Many of these can be used and adapted to beginning through intermediate levels.

RESOURCE A

THE DALCROZE INFLUENCE ON STRING PEDAGOGY

Emile Jaques-Dalcroze (1865-1950) was a student at the Conservatoire of Music in Geneva, Switzerland; studied with Leo Delibes in Paris and with Anton Bruckner in Vienna. He served as Professor of Harmony at the Geneva Conservatoire and became a dedicated educator, composer and conductor.

He felt that instilling an intrinsic knowledge and feeling for rhythm and tonality was absolutely essential and should be a basic goal for all who teach music whether instrumental or vocal. The aesthetic experiences such as the ability to perceive, to react, to express, to respond to music should be one of the primary goals in the teaching of music. His objective was to train the ear, mind and body to work together. All of these experiences and objectives should be presented in a game-like format which is attractive to the young student.

The Dalcroze approach is a visable expression and response to rhythm, meter, dynamics, tempos, form and melody. The teacher is able to see and hear how well students are reacting and developing. These musical concepts can be paced according to the progress being displayed. Songs like "Mary Had a Little Lamb," "Hot Cross Buns" and others in the "pre-Twinkle" period and progressing into Volume 1 "Twinkle," "Lightly Row," etc. (used in this text) would be appropriate in a Dalcroze-type program and an excellent preparation when transferring these concepts to the instrument.

There are three parts to this method: eurhythmics, solfegé and improvisation. Eurhythmics is a physical response to meter and rhythm and can be expressed in different ways such as marching, clapping, tapping a drum, swaying and tapping the foot. Solfegé (aural skills) is the development of inner hearing. Singing songs on pitch with words or syllables will teach tonal relationships. This can be effectively implemented even with young students at age two-and-one-half to three. They are able to match pitches, sing songs and coordinate this with rhythmic body movements. The ear-training games increase musical perception which results in a more sensitive response to the elements of timing, articulations, tone quality and phrase feeling. Improvisation is the creative part where students can freely express dynamics, tempos and rhythms with a variety of movements.

These internal concepts can be applied to the mental and physical aspects of playing a musical instrument. They assist in directing proper finger placements (pitch), bowing actions (rhythm) and keeping steady beats (meter). These concepts build excellent beginning left hand and bowing techniques. Eurhythmics and solfegé experiences also help to achieve music reading at a quicker rate and with greater accuracy.

Since this is a flexible program, teachers can use their own repertoire and work these into an interesting Dalcroze-type program. With this description of the Dalcroze method developing essential musical concepts, one can understand why this approach should be seriously considered as basic to musical learning.

RESOURCE B
PIZZICATO PLAYING

Pizzicato or plucking the string with the first finger of the right hand is suggested in the beginning stage so that the student can concentrate on the left hand position and finger placements while learning the notes and rhythms of the piece. Meanwhile, special bowing exercises are developing the various parts of the bow with a silent bowing program. Both are working on the same repertoire at the same time. Combining the left hand and bowing movements after each is functioning properly produces a solid start.

Pizzicato can be played without holding the bow, usually when playing longer sections. In shorter passages, the bow is held with the second, third and fourth fingers while the first does the plucking. The thumb is placed on the corner at the end of the fingerboard and the first finger plucks sideways for a clear, ringing sound. If plucked vertically, the string hits the fingerboard making a percussive and unmusical sound. Also, a harsh, brittle response will result when plucked too close to the end of the fingerboard or a soft and weak quality when too far down the fingerboard. Sometimes, however, these special sounds are requested by the composer especially in more advanced solo and orchestra music.

Notes that are to be plucked are marked pizz. (abbreviation for pizzicato) and arco when returning to play with the bow.

RESOURCE C

Chinrests

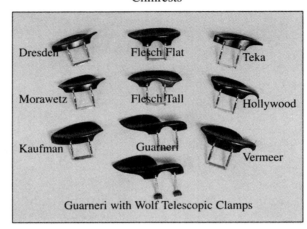

Guarneri with Wolf Telescopic Clamps

    The chinrests that are illustrated represent a sampling of some of the currently available styles. Their names may vary among suppliers and the shapes also vary slightly according to the manufacturer. However, these that appear in the photo are considered standard brands. If trying to find the right fit, select one that is most comfortable. It is advisable to request the local instrument supply store to allow a one-week trial (exchange) period. The teacher and student can work together to find the right combination of chinrest and shoulder rest or pad. When attaching the chinrest to the violin be careful not to allow it to rest against the tail piece.

Name-Material-Sizes

Dresden (low, medium cup) plastic, ebony, rosewood, boxwood. For 4/4, 1/2, 1/4, 1/8, 1/16 size violins.
Morowetz (large flat cup) ebony. 4/4, 3/4.
Kaufman (large flat cup) ebony, rosewood. 4/4, 1/2.
Flesch Flat (large flat cup centered over tailpiece) ebony, rosewood, boxwood. 4/4, 3/4.
Flesch Tall (large cup centered over tailpiece) ebony, rosewood, boxwood 4/4, 3/4.
Guarneri (medium cup over tailpiece) ebony, rosewood, boxwood. 4/4, 1/2.
Guarneri (with wolf telescopic clamps) ebony, rosewood, boxwood. 4/4, 3/4.
Teka (large cup) ebony. 4/4, 3/4.
Hollywood (large flat cup that fits over tailpiece) ebony. 4/4, 1/2.
Vermeer (large flat cup over tailpiece) ebony, 4/4, 3/4.

    Most of these can be attached without adjustments. However, if adjustments need to be made for proper fitting, it is important to know where and how these can be done.

The following are suggestions:

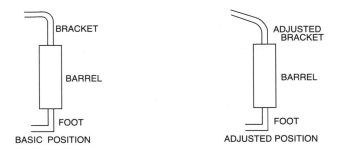

The bracket may need a slight angle adjustment to avoid cutting into the instrument. Best to have the local violin shop do it.

The barrel should be as long as possible to create a proper fit from top to bottom. Violin barrel has 23-29 treads. Viola has 35-40. A minimum number of treads should appear when chinrest is firmly in place.

The Wolf telescopic clamp eliminates the need for a chin rest with a special barrel size since it can adjust to any size violin.

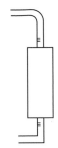

Wolf Telescopic Clamps.

For instruments that have a steep slant, the cork on the foot of a chinrest may require an adjustment when attached to the bottom edge on the back.

Shoulder Rests and Pads

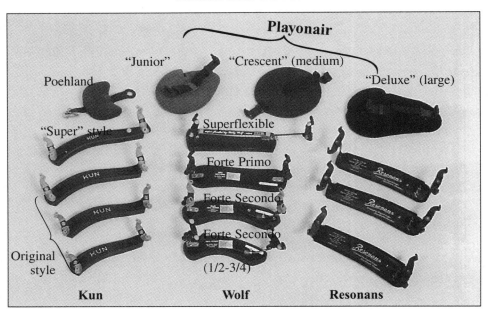

Kun Original: a crescent-shaped bar covered with a black sponge. The feet can be adjusted for height, width, pitch. Comes in two styles: The "original" has a wider range of adjustment giving longer use as the student goes up in size; the "super" model has adjustment capability which may be helpful in obtaining an exact fit. They also differ slightly in feel. Try them both to see which is most comfortable and workable. This is a very popular shoulder rest.

> Original available: 4/4 full size; 3/4 - 1/2; mini-size 1/16 - 1/4.
>
> Super available: 4/4; 3/4 - 1/2

Wolf Forte Primo: A curved bar covered with a sponge rubber pad. Feet can be adjusted for height, pitch. Has screw-on swivel legs. Sizes, 4/4, 3/4.

Wolf Forte Secondo (two are shown): A curved bar covered with a sponge rubber pad. Feet can be adjusted for height, pitch. Has screw-on swivel legs. Sizes 4/4 - 3/4; 1/2 - 1/4; 1/8 - 1/16.

Wolf Superflex: A curved bar covered with a sponge rubber pad. Feet can be adjusted for height, width, pitch, and tension. This can be adjusted to different size violins.

Shoulder Pads

Poehland: A crescent shaped firm pad concave in structure and covered with corduroy or velveteen. A rubber band loops over the corner of the violin bout and it has a leather strap with a hole to attach to end pin. Comes in full and small sizes.

Playonair: An inflatable non-slip suede finish material. It's soft yet gives firm support. Comes in different shapes and available in all sizes. Very comfortable.

Shoulder Rests

Resonans: A curved bar which tilts, covered in padded black velvet. Height is not adjustable, but available in different heights.

> 4/4, 3/4, 1/2 size violins (available in low (#1), medium (#2), high (#3) heights.
>
> 1/4 size violin (available in low, high).

> If necessary, the bar can be bent to fit curve in shoulder. Caution must be taken, however, not to displace the rubber feet, which may damage the varnish if exposed to the metal.

Kun Original: A crescent shaped bar covered with a black sponge. The feet can be adjusted for height.

> 4/4, 3/4, 1/2 size violins. Also, mini-size violins (1/16, 1/8, 1/4)

Kun Super: A more modern design than Kun original. Very adjustable for height and width.

> 4/4, 3/4, 1/2 size violins

Newsky: This shoulder rest comes in low, medium, high heights. 4/4, 3/4, 1/2, 1/4 size violins.

Shoulder Pads

Poehland Model C: A crescent shaped pad and concave in structure. Made of sponge rubber covered with corduroy or velveteen. It has a rubber band that loops over the corner of the bout and a leather strap with a hole to attach to the end pin.

Sponge (not shown): From 3/16 to 1 inch thick to fit 1/16 through full size violins. These may be made from a plain latex (not cellulose) kitchen sponge, cosmetic sponge or upholstery foam. It is held in position by rubber bands looped over the corners of the bouts to the tail button, or simply around the body of the violin.

Commercial Pads: These are specially cut commercial foam pads available to fit 1/16 to full size violins. They can be obtained at a local violin shop.

Descriptions of chinrests and shoulder pads from Southwest Strings Catalog, Tucson, Arizona.

Photos and additional descriptions of chinrests and shoulder pads from Kenneth Stein Violins, Evanston, Illinois.

CHINRESTS
(Lorraine Fink)

Chinrests come in many shapes and sizes, and in wood or other composition. A chinrest on any violin can be changed. One does not need to keep the one that came with the instrument. Chinrests that are very flat do not help hold the instrument securely, and those that have an extreme shape may not fit some players.

Most of the discomfort of chinrests, especially for children, is caused by the ridge on the edge cutting *across* the jawbone rather than nestling parallel to and in the soft tissue *behind* the jawbone and chin. This can usually be corrected by adjusting the angle of the violin to the head (body), often moving the scroll to the left. Virtually the entire ridge of the chinrest will be concealed by the jaw. Remember to keep the nose turned toward the strings.

A soft cloth held over the chinrest by a rubber band can soothe sharp angles of wood or the metal clamps. Bulky fabric such as corduroy stuffed with padding to cover the chinrest often disguises the problem of a badly positioned violin!

SHOULDER PADS OR RESTS
(Lorraine Fink)

The purpose of a shoulder pad is to secure the holding of the instrument. The most common error is that of using a support that is too thick or "high," supposedly to "fill up the space." A realistic appraisal of the area between a well-positioned shoulder and head reveals that, in addition to the depth of the chinrest and violin, there is usually less to "fill" than one might think!

Modern medical studies have established that violin playing "can be hazardous to your health." When no "anti-slip" device is used, it causes the shoulder to push up, the head to clamp down, and the back to get out of alignment. When a too-high shoulder rest is used it pushes the shoulder down, strains the head upward to accommodate the mass, and distorts the numerous muscles into dangerous postures. Those who reject even the soft almost denseless, cheap vinyl sponges (or latex upholstery sponge) are denying reality.

It is not unusual for children in violin sizes 1/16 through 1/4 and even larger to do well with a sponge (from 3/16 to 1 inch thick). When that is to be replaced with a commercial brand, begin by trying the lowest models that do not *wriggle* on the back of the violin. Be sure the violin is well positioned on the shoulder when the student tries different models.

Shoulder rests that attach to the edges of the violin are thought to allow for better tone since the violin back is left untouched. Many of the non-flexible rests have sufficient adjustment angles to fit the individual contours of the player.

RESOURCE D

PARTS OF THE VIOLIN AND BOW

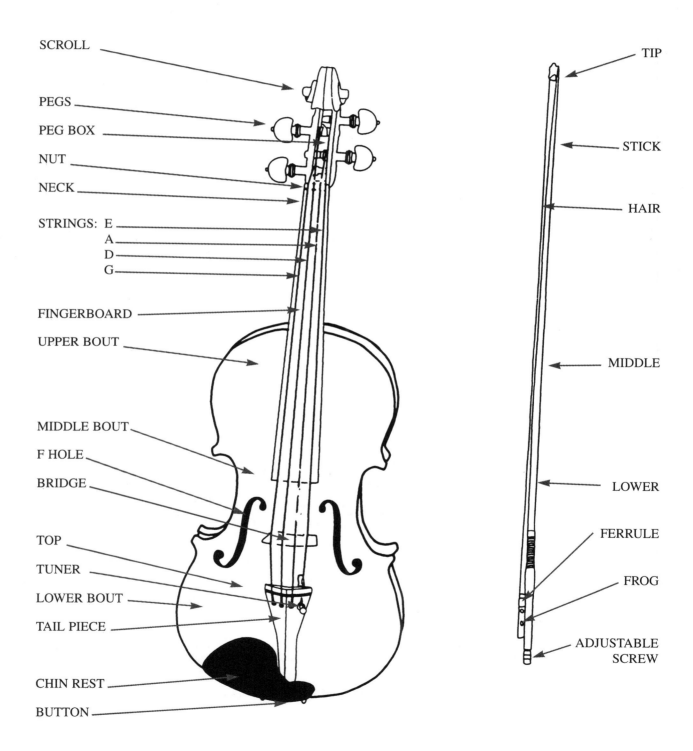

SCROLL

PEGS

PEG BOX

NUT

NECK

STRINGS: E

A

D

G

FINGERBOARD

UPPER BOUT

MIDDLE BOUT

F HOLE

BRIDGE

TOP

TUNER

LOWER BOUT

TAIL PIECE

CHIN REST

BUTTON

TIP

STICK

HAIR

MIDDLE

LOWER

FERRULE

FROG

ADJUSTABLE
SCREW

RESOURCE E

GLOSSARY OF TERMS USED IN TEXT

Accent (♪) - A stress or weight in the beginning of the note creating a louder sound.

Adagio - A slow and graceful tempo but a little faster than largo.

Allegretto - Moderate tempo. A little slower than allegro.

Allegro - A rapid, lively tempo.

Andante - A slower tempo than allegretto. Generally a moderately slow tempo.

Andantino - Not as slow as andante.

Arco - Play with bow. Usually follows a pizzicato passage.

Arpeggio - Chordal notes played separately.

A Tempo - Return to original speed.

Binary Form - A piece which consists of two different parts (e.g. A B).

Cadence - The concluding measure or measures of a sentence or the entire piece.

Chord - Three or more notes played at the same time.

Concerto - A piece containing several movements written for one or more solo instruments with piano or orchestral accompaniment.

Crescendo (◁) - A gradual increase in volume.

Decrescendo (▷) - Gradual decrease in volume.

Double Stop - Playing two strings (notes) at the same time.

Down Bow (⊓) - Bow is drawn from lower toward upper part of bow.

Dynamics - Indicates level of volume (e.g. *pp*-very soft; *p*-soft; *mf*-medium loud; *f*-loud; *ff*-very loud)

Etude - An exercise or study concentrating on a particular technique.

Flat (♭) - Note is a half-step lower.

Frog - Lower part of the bow.

Glissando - Sliding the finger from one tone or position to another.

Interval - Distance between two notes.

Key - The key is determined by the first note of the scale. Includes half and whole steps (intervals).

Largo - Very slow tempo with a sustained tone quality.

Lento - A relatively slow tempo. A little faster than adagio but not as fast as andante.

Lower Half - Part of bow from frog to middle.

Minuet - French dance played at a moderate tempo in triple meter (e.g. $\frac{3}{4}, \frac{6}{8}$).

Moderato - A moderate speed.

Movement - A complete musical section of a larger piece such as a concerto, sonata or symphony.

Natural (♮) - Eliminates a sharp or flat.

Pizzicato (pizz.) - Plucking a string or strings.

Repeat - A return to the beginning of a section (:‖) or repeat what is written between these two signs (‖: :‖).

Ritard (rit.) - Slow down the tempo. Usually at end of sentence or piece.

Scale - A series of notes within an octave range. Can be major, minor, chromatic.

Sforzando (sfz) - An accented note.

Sharp (#) - Note is a half step higher.

Slur (♩♩) - Playing two or more notes in the same bow.

Tempo - Rate of speed of a piece (e.g. andante, moderate, vivace).

Time Signature - Indicates meter of piece. The upper number indicates how many note values in a measure. The bottom indicates the kind of notes represented (e.g. $\frac{4}{4}$ - four quarter notes in a measure and each quarter note receives one beat. $\frac{6}{8}$ - six eighth notes in a measure and each eighth note receives one beat)

Tip - Top part of bow.

Trill - Quick and even alterations between two notes - the written note and the note above (e.g. ♩ tr)

Up-Bow (V) Bow drawn from top toward frog.

Upper Half - Portion of bow from middle to top.

Vibrato - A regular fluctuation of pitch produced by a coordinated motion of left fingers, hand, wrist, and arm creating expressive tone quality.

Vivace - A quick, brisk moving tempo.

KEYS - MAJOR AND RELATED MINOR SCALES

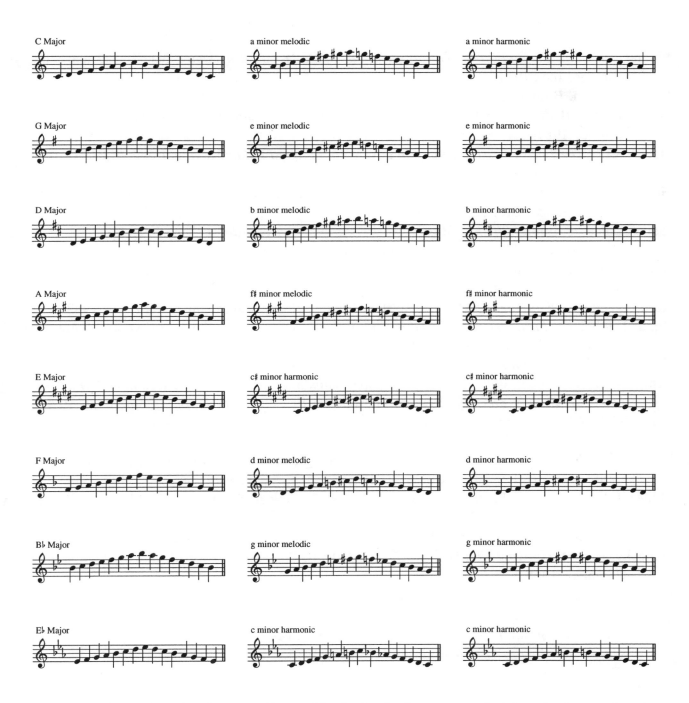

The melodic minor key is generally used in the beginning stage rather than the harmonic minor. The harmonic minor raises the seventh note of the scale ascending and descending creating an augmented second (1 1/2 steps) between the sixth and seventh notes and a difficult interval to reach. The melodic minor, raises the sixth and seventh note 1/2 step ascending and eliminates these when descending. Note patterns remain a half or whole step which is more comfortable to play

REFERENCES

Applebaum, Samuel. *First Position Etudes for Strings.* Miami, Florida: Belwin Inc. (Warner Bros.), 1984.

Findlay, Elsa. *Rhythm and Movement: Applications of Dalcroze Eurhythmics.* Miami, Florida: Summy-Birchard Inc., 1971.

Galamian, Ivan. *Principles of Violin Playing and Teaching.* New Jersey: Prentice-Hall, 1985.

Gelb, Michael. *Body Learning (Introduction to the Alexander Techniques).* London: Aurum Press Limited:1981.

Havas, Kato. *The Twelve Lesson Course in a New Approach to Violin Playing.* London: Bosworth and Co., Ltd., 1968.

Havas, Kato and Landsman, Jerome. *Freedom to Play: A String Class Teaching Method.* New York: ABI/Alexander Broude, Inc., 1981.

Jaques-Dalcroze, Emile. *Rhythm, Music, and Education. Revised Edition.* Translated by Harold F. Rubenstein. Redcourt, England: The Dalcroze Society, 1962.

Jones, Frank Pierce. *Body Awareness in Action (A Study of the Alexander Techniques).* New York: Schocken Books, 1979.

Karp, Theodore. *Dictionary of Music.* Evanston, Illinois: Northwestern University Press, 1983.

Kendall, John. *The Suzuki Violin Method in American Music Education Revised Edition.* Miami, Florida: Summy-Birchard Inc. 1985.

Klotman, Robert. *Teaching Strings.* New York: Schirmer Books, 1988.

Landis, Beth and Carder, Polly. *The Eclectic Curriculum in American Music Education: Contributions of Dalcroze, Kodaly, and Orff.* Reston, Virginia: Music Education National Conference, 1972.

Mark, Michael L. *Contemporary Music Education.* New York: Schirmer Books, A Division of MacMillan, Inc., 1988.

Müller, J. Frederick; Rusch, Harold W.; Fink, Lorraine. *Quick Steps to Note Reading.* San Diego, California: Kjos Publishing Company, 1979.

Müller, J. Frederick; Rusch, Harold W. *String Method.* San Diego, California: Kjos Publishing Company.

Perkins, Marianne Murray. *A Comparison of Violin Playing Techniques: Kato Havas, Paul Rolland, and Shinichi Suzuki.* American String Teachers Association, 1995.

Pernecky, Jack M. *Growing with Strings (String Method).* Chicago, Illinois: M.M. Cole Publishing Company, 1966.

Polnauer, Frederick and Marks, Morton. *Senso-Motor Study and Its Application to Violin Playing.* Urbana, Illinois: American String Teachers Association, 1964.

Rabin, Marvin and Smith, Priscilla. *Guide to Orchestral Bowings Through Musical Styles.* Madison, Wisconsin: University of Wisconsin Extension, 1984.

Reimer, Bennett. *A Philosophy of Music Education.* Englewood Cliffs, New Jersey: Prentice-Hall, Inc., 1970.

Rolland, Paul with Mutschler, Marla. *The Teaching of Action in String Playing: Developmental and Remedial Techniques for Violin and Viola.* Urbana, Illinois: Illinois String Research Associates, 1986.

Rolland, Paul. *Young Strings in Action.* Revised by Sheila Johnson. Farmington, New Jersey: Boosey and Hawkes, 1985.